Humorous satire stories told by Casey, a cat who reads minds and solves crimes travelling all over the world.

JOHN A. MEYER

'NUFF TO MAKE A
CAT
Laugh!

'NUFF TO MAKE A CAT LAUGH BOOKS!

'NUFF TO MAKE A CAT LAUGH BOOKS!

Paperback ISBN: 978-0-578-16284-3
Hardback ISBN: 978-0-578-16285-0

Library of Congress Control Number: 2015907701

PRINTED IN THE UNITED STATES OF AMERICA

Acknowledgments

Dedicated to Buddie, Mariam's silverpoint Siamese cat, whose endless curiosity, beauty, personality, and antics were the inspiration for this book.

This book would not have been possible without the support and encouragement of my friend, literary agent, and editor, Mariam Bartram, and her assistance in polishing this manuscript and nudging me to continue to write.

Casey

eow to you too! I am Casey the cat, named after some famous baseball player, John says, because he loves sports. I can read minds, anyone's and anything's. It is a gift. I am a very beautiful cat—most of us are—with a sparkling light gray coat, of course. My eyes are deep sea blue, and they are a great help in not only reading minds, but at times, interjecting "ideas" where I want them to be. I am on the large side, weighing about twenty pounds, but am excellently proportioned, because I am sinewy muscled throughout with great coordination, creativity, timing, and lots more than humans have ever heard or imagined. Might as well say I am not lacking in confidence a bit, and I have no modesty whatsoever. I am as good as it gets! Whatever you could imagine as being the greatest, I am all that and more! Yet, I still have many cat traits which are intrinsic and must be obeyed. If not for these traits, I would fly a jet fighter and free the world, but one of my cat traits holds me back. I don't like work. Not only that, I won't work. So for one insignificant cat trait, the world must plod along on its own. I have many other traits, ambitions, desires, wishes, dreams, and capabilities too numerous to paw down, or "write down" as humans say, and as you read on, you will find what they are. The main one is that I like a free ride, a clean house, yes, even love, and a man to live with who has a mind that is interesting, humorous, and malleable. (Don't get me wrong. I can read and instruct any mind, but for example, I will have nothing to do with the minds of the current leaders of the world.

That's their job, and sounds like too much work for me anyway.)
There are millions of other things I demand, and I will get to them
as we go along. It will be a great and fun ride! Cat's pajamas and all
that, don't you know?

It was a dark and stormy night. (Don't we all simply love
Snoopy?) It actually was, and I was completely lost and on my
own since I had just been dropped off a chicken truck going to
market. What's a kitten to do? All I could do was begin walking
and sniffing and then repeat the process. In about one minute I
heard some noise and looked up to see what it was. It was a human walking and making lots of noise and thinking all kinds of
thoughts. (It was then I realized I could read minds. The fall from
the truck must have hit the right spot and opened up the entire
world to me in millions of ways that I am still encountering every
day.) The human looked down at me and said, "Are you lost?"
(That was also the first time I laughed. I mean, here is a tiny kitten
in a watery, grassy ditch three miles from nowhere, and what does
it look like? Hell, no, I'm on my way for a pedicure, and my Rolls
will be along any second! Also, it was the first time I found that
I was sarcastic and had a sense of humor. I was hungry. I could
instruct people's subconscious to do what I wanted, and millions
of other things that would come to me by the jillions every second,
but for right now, let's get me out of the ditch, warm, and fed. The
other abilities I have will explain themselves or remain a mystery
to the reader depending on the reader's abilities.) Ahem.

The walker's name was John. He picked me up, sniffed me a bit,
and won my heart forever. He put me in his backpack, and we went
home. Upon arriving at his home, he put me on the table, dried me
off, and checked me for whatever he thought he should look for. He
gave me some carrot juice and chicken slices, and I almost laughed
again, because I knew this was not "cat food." Upon reading his

mind some more, I discovered he was very concerned about me, thought I was beautiful, and wanted a cat to guard his house. Huh? And, that it seemed like a good idea to take me to a doctor and get me up and into whatever kinds of shape cats must be in.

Next day off to the vet we went. I was scrubbed and examined, and this and that, and I was entirely happy. All the while keeping a straight cat demeanor and listening to all the minds of the people who were in contact with me. Fascinating! So much, and yet I knew all of it, including the various medical phrases or Latin terms that were being used. Even more fascinating was listening to John's mind as I was being examined. I knew instantly that I had found him, and that he had not found me. This guy needed help. Just what I wanted to springboard me to whatever I wanted do. He needed me to "gently guide" him in whatever way he was going.

John has good qualities. He's smart, strong, enthusiastic, humorous, caring, interesting, and sometimes smarter than hell, like a cat. Maybe that is why I liked him so much. Whattacat, John!

We went home, and John began immediately setting up the two things that he thought cats needed, a place for food and a place to eliminate the food. (At times John is very elemental. At times, oh, my heart, his middle name should be…anyhow, I digress.) We then went for a drive, which I loved, going all over where it would take me days with so many things to see and food everywhere. I could sleep at any time, and although I wasn't crazy about the radio stations, I would fix that in time. I didn't want to jolt the old boy too badly. Ha! Ha!

This was my beginning in the human world, falling off a chicken truck and John finding me, or me finding John. Some people compare it to Superman's start, and if I could fly, you would never think of Superman again. I knew I was off to do what must be done to get this whole show going, and I could not wait. John was there with me. How cat unlike of me to take John in. But his humor sold the deal. That sniff he gave me with his big schnoz didn't hurt either. Mew! Mew!

Top Cat Al

I know it is my duty as one of the leading, if not the leader, cat shrink to meow loudly and profanely about the way people and animals treat one another. They do a number on themselves as well, but I will meow and caterwaul. More on that later. First, I will comment upon and offer lead pipe solutions To solve the human condition, great writing by William Saroyan incidentally, and yes I can read all the best books. John doesn't know about that either. How could he? Believe me when I tell you that I can solve all human problems because only I can truly know something that you will never know. You may think you do, but you don't and you never will.

Case in point. Surviving the human condition is easier than trying to retain one you-know-who uncle. For many years, his idea of fun, besides getting loaded on catnip and sucking bird eggs, has been to sleep high in mind or altitude. Scream his cat brains out whenever he wants, and then jump on passing ravens or crows and make them go wherever he travels for free, anywhere. For European trips, Uncle Al uses whatever can hold him. He's getting pudgier now, and robins don't work so well anymore. To top it all off, yes, he calls himself the Top Cat. He will EAT the pilot if they don't go where he wants. Never pays. Each time he makes them wait until he is "finished." I have only mentioned the "high" lights, point being, can you imagine talking common cat sense into a guy like that?! Impossible! As the Perry Como song goes, it would be easier to make Al quickly "do you supper…nah," eat pork in an amusement park. As you can easily understand, the animal condition is much more complex than the human one. Now, to state the problem and then to solve it. Problem is, humans are going to hell in a hand basket, and smoking cigarettes with blue-tip matches and trying to light both at the same time.

Radio with John

I listen to the radio with John, but he doesn't know it. He thinks I am sleeping or having cat thoughts. I'm not. Today he was listening to a station, and he was laughing like crazy. Kind of reminds me of crazy Uncle Al. The station was playing, and I couldn't hear it all that correctly, the Rush Limbaugh show. This guy, Limbaugh, knew what to do and say about everything it seemed, no matter what. People would call in and say this or that, and Limbaugh would say, "No, no, tsk, tsk," and that would be that. Top cat, I call him. The humans call what we call top cats "president." No doubt about it, Limbaugh knew what to do about everything.

It seems the humans have all kinds of problems. How come? We cats don't have a one. We all act the same, except for me, and know exactly, innately, what to do in any given situation. Why can't the humans figure it out? Well, Limbaugh knows what to do. He hollers and laughs and says *do it that way or this way or hit the highway*. Again, I don't know what all these things really mean. I'm a cat, after all. I am only repeating them. But he sure sounds like a top cat to me, and he should be put in charge. His talking and hollering and what humans call laughing sounds exactly like what top cats do. I know a real top cat now who knows it all. Scary! Cats are scary enough, but when they say they know more than the rest, it even makes a cat nervous. The top cat I know meows real loud all the time, fights constantly, steals other's food, wants it all for himself, gets loaded on whatever, and sucks eggs whenever he can.

Sounds like crazy Uncle Al or worse. Al and his Raven Airlines are way ahead of top cat in travel, but each time old Al is really nice. Whereas, top cat never stops. I had to switch radio channels with my tail. John never noticed, since I switched it to another of what John calls a "BS" station. Again, I don't know what humans are really saying when they talk. I only repeat it to you. But I enjoy it, and besides, I only want to keep John happy and try to keep him from giving me two baths a week. I am one clean cat. It makes John happier than it does me. When he washes me, most of the water ends up on the floor, and when I meow loudly, I can hear him thinking, *Boy, I guess I am doing a good job now*. Like I always say, "And it hears." I almost said the cat, and made a tiny cat joke, repeating. I have to keep a close whisker on him. It's easy. John is often saying things, and then saying it wasn't him who said it. But it was. A guy named Shakespeare who? Well, it sure sounds good, and John has his brain packed with what he calls the Shakes. Hah! Can't fool a cat! John makes up the sayings, and then says, "This guy Shake whatever, said it." I get a kick out of it. Sometimes John says other things that he says came from the Bible. At that point, I have to purr loudly and meow a bit to calm him down. He sounds too much like top cat at tenor pitch, and even worse, good old Limbaugh. It is a common fault all humans have. Why can't they be like cats? Rhetorical. I know why, and I will tell you. They are stupid and ugly with bad genetics. Have you seen an ugly cat? I know Uncle Al comes close, or a cat that works, or a cat that is nervous, or that cannot get as much love as he wants? Never! We have it all! When I read John's mind at night, he realizes we are perfect, and the next day, he tries to give me a bath. It gives me a big cat laugh and so what? Last night I dined in the fridge and ate all his ice cream and lasagna. I have the best gig of any cat in the whole world. Well, almost. My hair is all over John's car, so I must help him get another one as if there are so many cars to choose from.

You know cats, at times, have a tough time making up their minds. I know for sure I won't let him get a motorcycle, or a pickup truck, or a coupe. I like lots of room and, of course, lots of class, and no road noise. Maybe a Jaguar, just kidding. Meow!

My Amazing Cat Abilities

*I*t was a dark and stormy night. That's something Snoopy would say, but I can do much better. I am a cat. The name, Casey, I have been given by the person who lives with me is Mr. Cat. His name is John. I like him very much, and I know he cares for me a lot. I know because I can read minds, not hard for our family. My mother told me that I had a very great gift that occurs in our family every so often. She said I must be careful with the gift because at times it needs much interpretation. Mom was right, but I have figured it all out, and I have a great time using all my cat-given gifts.

Right now, for example, I am writing down how I can look and listen to the world using my great capabilities. John showed me how to use the computer. I just read his mind while he's using the computer, and away I go. Literally! The best time to read his mind is when he is sleeping. (My mind-reading ability is increased when my whiskers are right next to or on the person whose mind I am reading. Some of the things I hear are too silly for a cat to understand, much less write about, but more about that later.) He thinks all kinds of stuff, and I only listen to or use what makes me happy. I learned about how to use a computer a long time ago when I would sit next to the computer while he was using and cussing at it. It made me laugh so hard that I almost fell off the table. All I could do was say a mellow "Meow" and John would look at me and pet me, and then cuss some more. At times it was too funny, and I had to leave the room for fear he might overload the laughing part of my cat brain. All I do when it is overloaded is meow louder, and I didn't want to disturb him.

To describe me outside of my abilities to read minds, with or without whiskers, I am a very beautiful Siamese cat. My athletic abilities freak John out and make him laugh. (He says, "Haw, haw, haw," and I can hear his mind say that he wants somehow to get me to play pro football. Whattanut!") My eyes are China blue, and if I tried at all, I could hypnotize people and animals, too. I can sing some songs if I try, and I sometimes sing along with John during "The Star-Spangled Banner" when Kate Smith sings. He is crazy about me when I do that! He tried to get me to sing some Sinatra. I read his mind, and he was also thinking about having me make records so he could make money off my singing. (I have to keep a close whisker on him. That way I know what he is going to do before he does. Wink. Wink. I don't want to become a working cat at any rate. Right now, I am enjoying being a cat writer.) My other abilities are common to other cats. Although I can't speak any kind of human language, I let my tail, ears, paws, eyes, and of course, a well-placed and mellow-sounding "Meow" do my talking for me. All the stuff I hear people say is ridiculous. It makes John laugh so hard that I fear he may forget about me and want to be around humans in place of me. Not to worry. When he is sleeping, I listen to his mind with my whiskers on his head, the absolute best way to read minds, and I know he wouldn't ever part with me. In fact, he thinks he may live longer than me or have to take me to a cat doctor for some kind of cat problems, and that worries him. I make a low purr in his ear, and he actually smiles in his sleep. He makes me smile a lot as well. When he rubs me under my chin, he says I smile like a Chinese person. Oh, yes, my other great quality is that I have a lovely smile. (I have not told you all of my qualities. Cats must be mysterious, you know! No problem there, as you are witnessing what I am doing now.)

About once a week, John gives me a bath. Scary! I hide, but sooner or later, he picks me up and into the tub we go. Afterward, I enjoy a towel rubdown massage. John is worried I will make the house smell like a cathouse. I would like to tell him sometimes that his smell is worse than mine. Well, actually I do tell him, but it is in cat talk. Sometimes I think that he almost understands me really. Then again, if he really did begin to understand me, he would probably just want me to sing Sinatra songs. Sometimes I worry about him as well. I don't know what he would do without me. Maybe I should contact my all-knowing mom. I have so many relations that maybe every few years, we should just replace me with another lookalike Siamese. They must be able to mind-read. However, they must also be beautiful and be able to write books. (Don't think it will happen anytime soon. My greatest talent may be in taking a bath so much.) Sigh... I must not let human foibles make me sad. Once it did, and I started to lose some hair. John thought I had some kind of a bug, so off to the cat doctor we went. Not nice, so much fear emanating from the cat place where he took me. John was scared also, so I had to purr to calm him down. He told the doctor I was losing hair, and what did that mean exactly? I read the doctor's mind, and he was afraid John was going to pick me up and run out through the wall. John was more nervous than I was. Seeing him like that calmed me down, and I realized all he wanted was to keep me one happy cat. My hair grew back right away. (Reading minds can be good, or not so good.) John may be better than I give him credit for, despite those baths. At times, he thinks and acts a lot like a cat.

I am extremely well fed. I have learned how to get into the fridge, and so I eat whatever and whenever I so desire. John has no idea I have this talent. Even when he came in the kitchen and my tail was sticking out of the fridge, he just went, "Haw, haw, haw," and helped me out and wiped off my whiskers. (It's so dark in the fridge, and when the door is closed, the light goes out. I guess that puts to rest the great question of "Does the light go out when the fridge door is closed?" Or, maybe I am guilty of watching one too many *Three Stooges* movies. Actually, one is too many! They give me a cat headache, and I make John turn the channel. I told a small cat fib, omission really. I can, at times, make John do what I want. Tell you how later!)

As usual, John takes me for a ride once or twice a day. Very nice. So much fun to see all the country, and we can do it so much faster than I ever could alone. People look at me and laugh and point, and that makes John laugh, and then, that makes me happy as well. We all have a great time laughing and talking. As usual, John was wondering how he could make money out of me by driving around. Sometimes I just want to "Meow!" really loud in his ear. But he can't hear very well as it is, and if he did get more money, he would think of some way to spend it on me. I know that. I read his mind, and he was thinking about taking a plane trip with me, but he was worried that I might not like it, or get hurt, or it might scare me very badly. I don't know, so I contacted one of my cat buddies, and he told me that all kinds of commotion breaks loose on an airplane. He said it was a nutty invention and surely no place for cats! Cousin cat Al went on an airplane trip and really let 'er go as my buddy said. Guess old Al let out about a three-minute primal cat scream, and the trip was called off. It became a big mess. (Al can't read minds, and about all he can do is raise hell. He's great at that! Al gives cats a bad name. He needs a bath, too.) The cat jury is still out on plane rides. If I had to get on a plane, I would behave if John really wanted to go, but it doesn't sound like a very fun time to this cat.

I am guilty of watching TV. I know, like most cats, I should be looking out the window, or sleeping in the sink, but I don't do that. I'm a way smarter cat than that! I have learned to use the channel changer, and I watch TV whenever I want. While watching Animal Planet, I saw a cat that weighed about a thousand pounds! He lived in Africa and for no other way to put it, he was meaner than hell, and scary too! I could pick up a few of his thoughts telepathically, and some of the other cat thoughts as well—not very nice, to put it mildly. All they did was eat whatever they came upon. It got so boring, they ate each other. One big cat of some kind looked into the camera, and I could see deeply into his mind by looking into his eyes. Place your bets that whoever was taking a picture of him was shortly dinner for that cat, or he was hidden in an army tank.

Give me a Clint Eastwood film any day! I like Clint and the way he talks, and in one movie, he had a dog. Okay, he treated the dog nice, and I could tell Clint would treat me just as nice, as well. (Better not tell John, or he will probably try to sell me to Clint. Then, steal me back, and who knows what? Like I say, sometimes John worries me.) Many of Clint's movies are in San Francisco. I know John likes it there because when he is asleep, he dreams of going there and taking me with him. He wants to take me to a bar and let me walk on the bar and have a sip of a drink there. Maybe I will, and maybe I won't. He also wants to take me other places and show me around. He is so proud of me. What can I do but give him what he wants, most of the time, and take a bath once a week. I better not let him see that horrible big cat movie, or that may give him bad dreams about cats. I must protect him from bad dreams.

We listen to radio at night. John likes the radio station Coast to Coast. I like it too, sometimes. They talk about aliens, outer space, mind readers (ahem), time travel, and you name it. One night they had a special program for cats, my favorite episode. The guest said how wonderful cats were, and of course, I agree. He went on to say that he had cats all his life, and that he could teach them anything he wanted. I was starting to get worried about now. He went on to say if you can make a five-hundred-pound tiger jump through a fire hoop, you can make a house cat (I didn't like that reference) do just about anything. He said he had a book out on how to train cats and make them do all sorts of things. About this time, I could tell John was starting to wake up and was going to want to write down the phone number. Things were getting complicated. That's all I wanted was to have John trying to make me do tricks, and trying to make money off my talents. I just gave John a small "Meow" and reached over with my tail and turned the radio off before he woke up any more. He went back to sleep, dreaming of me jumping through fire hoops before thousands of people in some stinky tent. No, thank you! Just the thought of all the thoughts in those other animals' heads would drive me bonkers.

Wait until I tell you about the time we went to the zoo. Then again, I might not. Imagine a ten-ton elephant getting up on a rubber ball and making a silly noise and wishing with all his great heart that he could see his parents again or go back to where he truly lived… too many painful memories. Tip of the iceberg, as humans say…

Life of a Mind-Reading Cat Psychologist

*I*t's football season playoffs, and I love it! I get to sing "The Star-Spangled Banner" about ten times in the next seven days. That and watching John go nuts and act like my crazy Uncle Al on catnip! John says with my tremendous speed, strength, and intelligence that I could be a great kickoff cat. No thanks! My tail would not hold up. Once my tail is gone, how can I communicate with John and tell him how I'm feeling or what I want? When he is asleep he sometimes grabs my tail and moves me around. I put my whiskers near him and read his mind and find out why. It is mainly because he just likes to feel what he calls my mink coat. He has told me that anybody born wearing a 24/7 mink coat that never wears out is very lucky. Throw in my two-inch lashes on these big blue eyes and four-inch whiskers and VA VA VOOM! You have a beautiful cat!

Today John is going to take me with him when he does his errands and goes to wash his clothes at the laundromat. About time! When he goes inside, he puts me in my cat bag, and it is a lot of fun. I stick my head out and people say the nicest things to me. John tells them how wonderful and beautiful I am and that I cost him $1,000. Once, he said, "For $1,001, he's yours. I'm having a hard time giving him a bath and for a thousand-dollar cat, you would think he should behave when it's bath time." The person smiled, and I knew he was thinking about actually paying John. Now, John is a big kidder, but I know he wouldn't sell me for any amount of money because I can read his mind.

Sometimes he wishes other people could have a great cat such as myself. It won't happen. Too many cats out there like my crazy Uncle Al and cousin Petunia. All they want to do is get loaded on catnip and chase a stupid laser red dot around on the floor, and that's just for starters. All so boring to me... I know Al needs a trip to the vet, wink wink, but he lives outside and the USMC couldn't catch him. He sleeps in the trees and the big cat in the sky only knows where else. When I see him, he usually has bird feathers stuck in his whiskers and chunks of fur missing. He won't behave in the slightest, and I won't let him in the house. Now, there is a cat that needs a bath and a dose of salts. Al is like most cats I have met. They are not $1,000 cute. Once John said I was a $1,500 cat. The person was very impressed, and I gave him my best Chinese smile and a small meow, so happy he thinks I'm that valuable to him, again, because I can read his mind. Ahem!

Cat Thoughts

*I*t's quite simple really. I am a cat that can read minds. Not as good as being a Siamese cat, but it breaks up the boredom, and it will help, John, my buddy, will buy some better food if this book sells. I don't have a favorite kind of food. I am one of those cats that doesn't care. John feeds me mainly beer, chicken, and potato chips. If he knew what I do and can do, he would take me to Hollywood in an instant and try to make money off me. In reading John's mind I can tell he almost knows that something is "going on" with me, but then I meow, look at him, and tweak his mind a bit. (Yes, I can mind-meld as well.) He goes on thinking of the solar system, the football game, or I just tune out. There's only so much a cat wants to know.

I can't just tell you all at once what I do, but I will take you through and introduce you to the things I can do, and you will like it very much. If you want to find me and take me to Hollywood, be careful. I know what you are thinking, and then there is mind-melding, which could leave you back on the farm. My grandfather used to tell us little cats: "Behave or you will be back on the farm." It confused me a bit when he said that, because at the same time, I was becoming aware of my mind-reading abilities. I was listening to what he was meowing, okay, "saying," and at the same time I was "listening" to his mind. His mind and what he was saying did not agree. Same thing with humans, only they are a lot more confusing just because they have tried to become smart.

Cats are naturally smart. We are the best. Cats just want to see, at any rate, some action and have humans or things in motion to give them something to look at. You will find out, and even if you don't agree, we don't care. We have other fish to fry. I must admit sometimes I use expressions humans use. I can't speak like a cat to you, so most of the time, I will speak like people. I will use only English. I can speak every language of every person and every animal and so what. I get the biggest kick out of what John says when somebody pulls in front of him while he is driving—that and a lot more. I may also get John a brand-new car when this book goes big because he wants a Mercedes with leather seats, he thinks, mainly for me. He laughs when he thinks about a stupid cat with Asian heritage riding around in a German car, driven by an Irish guy who knows if he can just find the right cat training book, he can make a million with me in Hollywood. As I say, I have to watch him.

So, let me tell you the story of what has been going on in the mind of the smartest being on the planet, not exaggerating a bit. I know some cats who can do a bit of what I can do, but they would much rather stare at a bug, or eat a bird, and then meow all over the place. When one compares cats to humans, many who have so much, they would rather eat Oreo cookies and watch sitcoms and do "whatever." (Don't like the word "whatever," but I must realize to whom I am writing. I know you want to get to the juicy stuff.)

Today began as usual. I have to keep a sharp eye and mind on John at night. He listens to Coast to Coast and gets some wild ideas. They talk about everything, and one guy was talking about training lions. He was a Clyde Beatty type. As I was reading John's mind, listening to the radio, and doing cat math—more on that later—John was slowly waking up and going to write down the phone number of the training book. Forget that! I could work around it quite easily, but I just stuck my tail in his ear, hit the off switch, and John fell back to sleep. If I attempt to alter his mind, he may forget about the Mercedes and the leather seats, and I would really like to walk around in a Mercedes on leather seats. I must have been around humans too long. Most cats will settle for just sitting on your breakfast while you are in the other room, but not me. Not to worry, I also keep a close eye on my abilities. John needs me to help him go the straight and narrow. Getting a quarter-million-dollar car to have a cat sit on leather seats is just the beginning. He has ideas of taking me to Hollywood, breeding me (oh my goodness, no more discussion on that subject!), leaving me with the "relation" while he goes off to who knows where (well, I really know, but I won't let him), getting another human to stay with him, or going to live with another one. Getting me a buddy?! That's enough! You can see some of the problems I have. Most are solved by a quiet meow or hiding. John wants to know where I am all the time. He thinks I am continually trying to escape. I'm not, exactly the opposite, but it helps me control him. Not too long ago we went to the park for a ride, and I jumped out when we parked. I read John's mind immediately, and he was thinking to get a leash on me and paw shoes. Forget that too! I just got back in the car. John winked at me, and I could not read his mind completely. Hmmm, sometimes I wonder about him. I am proud to say I am a service cat. Ha! Ha! John thought it would be a good idea, so that he could take me with him wherever he goes. He went to a tailor, and they fitted me with a great jacket that is lightweight, stylish (I helped with the design, ahem...), and has pockets. When he is asked by people, "What is this cat all about?" John tells them a different story every time. I am amazed. He has brains like a cat with a much better sense of humor. We are so serious, and talk about making a cat laugh. I have to let out some pretty fat meows when we get outside. John winks at me sometimes when I do. That's okay. He thinks he knows that I am up to something, but he will never get that Clyde Beatty cat training book. It is the book or the Mercedes, take his pick. It's easy to distract him. He likes me to meow, and then sometimes he meows back. Who cares? I can't watch him all the time, and when I don't, I "catch" him thinking about stuff that ruffles my fur. (I told you I would have to revert to human lingo from time to time, so stay forewarned.)

His latest great idea was going to Thailand. No, thank you! They eat us cats there, you know. It would be a big struggle for me. I weigh about thirty pounds, beautiful all over, with shiny, scotch tapioca-colored hair. Too much! They would probably kidnap the plane before it landed, just like the plane that mysteriously vanished not too long ago. I am worth more than a stupid plane. Worth more than solar systems at least, but even great cats like me like what they want, and I like John's jokes. Well? What do you like, dear reader, Twinkies and shoe polish? I like to laugh, and I like my life, and John is as good as it gets. At nights when John has troubling dreams, I purr and tell him all is wonderful. It makes him so happy, and he immediately thinks of me in a Mercedes, and I have to put a pillow over my head so he won't hear me laughing. It's so easy to make him happy, and for him to make me happy as well. But, Thailand, seriously?! That is where I will put my paw, or paws, if need be, down. I don't want to go into regime changing. Just to think of having to hang around with those slobs would upset me a lot. Yes, I have feelings. You would be upset as well if you knew people would be trying to eat you every second of the day. I mean, I could deal with it, but why waste my talents.

Ha! Ha! I know what you are thinking as well. So knowing that I know what you are thinking, please think about that while I continue. Every day, I watch the news, listen to the radio, go to the movies, ride around, and go where John does. I'm pretty much with him all the time, or keeping an eye out for him, or making sure he doesn't get out of control when I am not there. I also have some friends who

I see from time to time and do stuff on my own. I know I can't control the entire environment, so I must be careful because I am too beautiful, smart, and happy to leave where I am. Not that I haven't thought of many other things, but humans are useful. I can't drive a car, fly a plane, or catch a pigeon a day to eat, and lots of other things, so John comes in handy. Sometimes I must be careful what I think when I am around John. When I get a faraway look, I think it may be possible for him to have an idea of what I am thinking. If I am thinking about going away, he may pick up on it and get the Clyde Beatty book when I am not paying attention. (Probably this is the only thing I might fear even an iota.) I think he knows that, as well, and he is kidding me a little. He likes to kid me, and sometimes it works. But I like to be kidded, too. It's all great with Uncle Al, the biggest kidder cat I know. 'Nuff to make a cat laugh!

Football

I love to watch football games and have John pet me while he watches the game with me. The faster the action, the faster he pets me. Whew! One guy ran back a kickoff for a touchdown, and it was all I could do to hang on to the rug so he wouldn't use me for a football and throw me at the TV. Like I meow, I have to keep a close eye on that guy. After John watches the game and goes to sleep (sometimes in the first quarter), he dreams about football, and sometimes cheerleaders—talk about fantasy! I can only stand so much and then I turn up the volume or purr in his ear, and then he wakes up and takes me for a ride. How much of a good time can a cat stand? In the car, on goes the game, and he listens to that for a while, and then it is over to the music channel that I have conveniently programmed, and then off to his favorite restaurant. He takes me in his backpack, and if anyone asks he says I am a care cat. Boy, am I ever! I saw a movie about shape shifters, and I wish I could do that. In effect, I have John running around doing most of the things I want, but there are some things he can't do. Not many, but even a cat has their limitations. Like Eastwood says, a cat has to know his limitations. I know mine. Now I have to worry about everybody else.

Today was a "very important" football game. John celebrated by falling asleep in the first quarter, and I had to wake him and get him directed. (So he would pet me some more and yell at the screen so much that it would even make a cat laugh. I mean, sometimes I have to leave the room.) He played football in college, so he thinks he can still play. Well, he knows he can coach, for sure. He did that as well. To listen to him yell at the TV, you would think he is on the field or in the huddle or in the locker room. But quickly, he goes to the fridge and cools himself down with one of his concoctions. He asks me if I want some of that swill, but I hardly ever do. Tastes funky. I leave that to my Uncle Al, who will drink seawater mixed with vodka and go, "Yea, yea, hip, hip, hooray!" Believe me, if Uncle Al was human, and sometimes I think he is, he would be the best football player in the world. Al does it all and in high gear. He even sleeps that way. Once I heard him talking about cheerleaders, and I had to leave the room. He was purring, meowing, and screaming at the same time, and showing in no uncertain terms what he would do on a date with the cheerleaders. (I think he meant all twelve at once!) It was too much for me, and I didn't want to make a mess on the carpet, so I went outside. Must remind myself to put one of John's tranquilizer pills in Uncle Al's zoom zoom drinks and try to slow him down. Uncle Al is all cat, tomcat, alley cat, big cat, bad cat, funny cat, clever cat, crazy cat, of course, and just plain, well, all cat with a capital C. Lots of fun, but don't invite him to a party of any kind unless it's held outside on about one hundred acres of land near the ocean, and make sure all the tractors are locked up real tight. Because that's how Al will be—real tight. More to come about Uncle Al. Just thinking about him makes me nervous, and writing about me would get me arrested if I wasn't a cat.

Super Bowl Football Game

So exciting to watch the Super Bowl! We waited anxiously for a whole month to see it. I double love it because John pets me constantly during the game—the faster the game, the faster the petting. At the very end of the game, I thought I was going to get a free cat ride across the room. (He has never thrown me in frustration, only in fun, and then I land on the couch or bed.) He left the room when Seattle had the ball on the five-yard line with three plays to go (and I thought cats in heat made a lot of noise), went to read a book, and turned off the TV. When he found out New England had actually won the game on a last-second play, he had what we cats call a cat fit. He didn't know what to do. So much emotion! That is why sometimes you will see a cat running around in circles in the house or wherever. It is because they are having an emotionally filled cat-fit time. It took him a few days to get over it, and I understand completely. To have your team win and lose twice in thirty seconds in the Super Bowl is too much. It still bothers him, but he doesn't throw any more yelling fits. Wow! He let out a big one! There was nothing in his mind but confusion. It was a white screen. I had to help him and do what I do best, so I rubbed my tail across his shin, and he settled down and took me for a ride. We listened to music, but sports were out that day.

I felt sorry for the old boy. Might be hard on his ticker and then what would I do? Oh, I know what to do, but I like him so much. I think he is the closest thing to a cat I will ever find in a human without a lot of looking around. (If he would only quit trying to think of schemes to send me to Hollywood.) It's so hard for humans to be perfect like cats. We are perfect and so beautiful. If they would put the steering wheel closer to the gas pedal, I think I could do without John, after he buys me a car, of course. I would also have to get some kind of a hat that would make me look human. Then again, I have seen some pretty strange humans driving around. I don't know what kind of a car I would get, but it would be a sturdy one. I would tint the windows so people could not see in, and of course, if I was pulled over, there are things I could do with the officer's mind that would make him let me go immediately. Since John taught in prison, I know a lot about police, and it seems that many of them already have lots done to their mind. If you are a policeman reading this, I do not refer to you, because most would never read about the most earth-shaking phenomenon in the world—me. At the risk of being tawdry, I know that they would be reading other types of cat books... ahem. Which brings to mind, why are humans so caught up in their naked bodies and what they do to each other with their bodies? After one second of half-hearted thought, the answer is too obvious. I won't bother telling you, and I should not have spent one second figuring it out. Ahhhh, time for my nap.

Okay, back to sports talk—John's favorite conversation subject. Basketball is now the sport that replaces football. I enjoy that sport also, and track as well. Can you imagine how high a cat could jump, how far and fast a cat could run, and on and on? We don't care at all. Humans talk for hours about how to shoot a ball, hit a ball, chase a ball, catch a ball and ball, ball, ball. I don't mind, and it has its moments. But if John didn't pet me constantly when there was "high action," I don't think I would be as interested. I am tempted to say I might be interested in the *Sports Illustrated* swimsuit issue, but I am not writing about the naked human and seeing it in various and contorted poses. If I did, it would only be to see the female body. I see the male body plenty, and sometimes too much for my cat eyes. I mean, why don't they clean up like we cats always do? They spray themselves, and it doubles whatever they are trying to spray away. If that isn't bad enough, they try to spray us. I must say John never does that, and he is very clean. I had to "suggest" to him how great it was to be clean, and he trained up nicely. However, at times when he gets out of the shower and sees me, he says, "Now are you happy?" and gives me a sly poker grin. Like I said, I have to keep a close eye on that guy.

South of the Border

I love music. Sinatra, Deano Martino, and the like is what this cat calls music. They played with the best bands and had the best orchestration and the absolute number one best writers ever, like ever! Fantastic lyrics. The writers of those lyrics do not get their just due. Simply put, they were up there with the Shake. I know they would agree. So does John. He just heard the song "South of the Border," and it tugged at his heart so much that he booked a trip to Mexico. I hardly made a meow. Off we went.

Acapulco, here we are. What a great place to stay, with the ocean view from our villa on the third floor, and the run of the house. That's my personal favorite. Actually all I do is run and get in the backpack and "suggest" to John what he would like to do. Love it! All on his own thought, John decided to take some kind of a fishing sightseeing cruise. Oh, goody! Seasick pills were passed all around, and then he bought a bottle of Patrón to help whomever needed it on this cruise. We left at five in the morning, and some of the passengers were kind of "sleepy." Also some looked kind of seedy, and I could tell they weren't here for the fish or the view. What were they here for? Monkey business, you think? I gave them a quick mind scan, and I was absolutely right, as usual. John was aware, too, and he put an Irish smile on his face and kept looking at the coast bobbing up and down. Boy, am I glad I took those pills!

I could not believe—well, really I could, but you know some-times you have to say that—that these three guys were going to hook up with a large ocean liner coming to dock and take it over. Yes, me laddy, ship stealing on the high seas. Aargggggghhh! Their plan was to use this sightseeing boat as a foil to get close so that it would be in its way, and then it would have to stop. When it did, they would get on board with help from their cronies on the ship, and carry out their plan. The old pirate plan, "Give us the money, or we ruin your honey." (That's how they talk, not me.)

I told John their plan, and he succinctly said, "Now what?" ('Nuff to make a cat laugh, but I had to keep a steady hold on the wheel...of something.) The three scoundrels were sitting close to-gether, and John brought out the "da da de da," the Patrón. (I know Jimmy Van Heusen could have written something better, but so what? I know he would say that. He wasn't jealous.) After all they were "men." This was the ocean. And what else is there? You got it, booze and Sinatra. John said something that woke up who needed to be. Three nice-looking women were obviously not there to fish, so he poured, while I purred (trying to get a "Way to Try" from Van Heusen), and they were very gracious and thankful. The would-be boat takeovers were sitting across the cabin from them and smiled appreciatively. (I mean, beauty rules; just look at me... Okay, smile.) After John had poured the lady a goodly portion of Patrón, one of the scoundrels said, "How about us?" John said, "Certainly, gentle-men, I just didn't know if you wanted to wake up or stay asleep. Let me pour you a booster to open your windows to the world." They frowned. I said, "Easy, Shakespeare, they don't even read stop signs." Three glasses appeared from the cabin, because by now the aura of these three creeps had invaded the entire crew and its pas-sengers. The men told John, "Pour!" (That is not a recommended way to talk to John.) He did pour, but before he did, he dropped in a double dose of knockout crud pills that he always carries for occasions such as this. They chugged the first serving and called for more. John poured quickly, as did their eyes and the sound of the glasses on the boat floor. Everyone on board knew these men were up to no good, and the United States Coast Guard just happened to be in the vicinity. Hummmmm. (Just happened?) They arrested the three men immediately and told everyone that those three men were well-known pirates throughout the world who had created much havoc and death wherever they went. They told us we were lucky that they "fell asleep." They also arrested all the men on the ocean liner, and it was a tremendous coup for ocean security.

Meanwhile, the three ladies were wide awake and enjoyed watching the creeps passing out, the Coast Guard coming on board and arresting the weirdos and questioning everyone, and they asked for more Patrón. "Sure," John said as he poured and I purred. All were happy, but not much fishing was done. So exciting to talk about the pirates, the mysterious passing out, and such things, and of course, I walked around the boat and caught their attention. I did my best—well, almost; after all, it was five in the morning—and my cat act on the high seas kept everyone completely delighted. We returned to shore around noon, I think.

The only watches around there were the Rolex kind. John and I went to a fabulous restaurant, and the three charming ladies came with us. I noticed they were wearing Rolex watches, and John was sporting only a bony wrist and his big Irish smile. Who do you bet on? Just a cat kidding around; "awctually" John's wrist and wallet are too skinny for a Rolex!

It was an outdoor veranda with a complete view of the ocean. The wind and smell from the ocean were as good as only that smell and feel can get. A soft wind wrapped around all of us, and sometimes at that time I wished I 'wasn't a cat. The charming ladies (I took a quick look into their minds and found out they were just slumming millionaires. So funny, even for me... 'Nuff to make a cat laugh!) We were having a great time. John had requested Sinatra music with a, ahem, small monetary inducement. All of us on this beautiful ocean veranda were having the time of our lives. Soon, John went on the stage and did some of his comedy shtick. I mean, even Frank has to take a break. Me, too.

Off to the side of the stage, I noticed a lurking presence. All smiles, but the eyes never stayed still. They were constantly surveying the entire area. They settled in on John. I gave them a quick mind read, and it read that there was trouble. The pirates were on land as well, and they were vengeful. I glanced over to where the three ladies were, and they were gone. I took a look to where the greaseball pirate was and saw that the three "ladies" had him in handcuffs. John noticed it as well, went over, and everything was explained. The ladies were actually federal agents posing as slumming millionaires. Tough job, I have to add. The entire situation was explained by the federal agents, and it was a fantastic story. Don't you think? John was kind of confused, so we went back to the room, and John grumbled. So funny to see him that way, don't you know? As John was sleeping there was a knock on the door, and I had to meow in John's ear so he would hear it. He opened the door, and all three agents came in with smiles and Patrón, and then put him in handcuffs. John said he never had a better time. I could say, "'Nuff to make a cat jealous," but I won't.

Coast to Coast

I hate Coast to Coast. No problem. Just hit the third button on the left with my paw, and off it goes. John is sleeping with the radio on, thinking he is learning about great mysteries, while he is "awctually" keeping me awake from what I like, and that is to do what I want when I want. I also have a responsibility to John. Keep him asleep. Sometimes Coast to Coast bothers him, and he tries to call them and says all kinds of sailor talk, but he can never find the number at three in the morn. So, I just drag my tail across his face or arm, one quick meow, and then walk lightly over him to the other side, and that usually calms him. He thinks he is following me down to the beach or something pleasurable. For now it works, and when it comes to Coast to Coast, I will get that program off no matter what. I may even throw a meow fit, and then John will "have" to pet me and calm me down, and off goes that station. Even sports stations are better. Like I say, running this railroad can be tough. Wink.

Last night we both had a great sleep. I was having an exciting cat dream, and John was just trying to stay calm. He was listening to the ball game, and somehow Coast to Coast came on. (I can't do it all by myself.) I even listened for a few minutes, and then I knew it was another nutcase spouting world domination or here come more aliens to get you. Brother! Way too much! Before I could turn off the radio, John was stumbling around trying to phone in to cuss out whomever. On come the lights, trip to the can, some cussing, and finally the phone. Finally, he got a number and called in. More cussing followed. Now, I have to report what happened.

John was ready to put me in the car and find where Coast to Coast broadcasted so he could choke them. He soon got bored and drank some carrot juice (which I told him to get) and went back to sleep.

Now what was I to do? I walked around and checked the doors and windows and smelled all to make sure things were as they should be. (Smelling and sniffing are so important. My clumsy cousins, the dogs, are always woofing and huffing and pretending they are smelling up a storm, but me and mine can get much more done in much less time without all the drama...harrumph... More time for us to smile as well, especially at our "cousins.") All was fine, so I took three steps and jumped six feet in the air and launched myself about sixteen feet right on John's bed with nary a noise or any way of knowing I had landed about seven inches from John's body. John "sensed" something. I can't believe he has any sense, but that proved it, and he inched his hand toward me and rolled me over and growled. Since it was three a.m., I had to let him pretty much do what he wanted. This time he was just checking to see if I was safe. Brother! Sometimes I have to keep a real close eye on that guy. Sometimes! After all, I have my standards, and John is the one who pays for them. I can't let him get hurt or do anything that would interfere with my comforts. Good thing my comforts are good for him as well. Sometimes too good. Sometimes I wonder...

We made it through the night. I was very happy and did my usual morning inspections of the house, and I noticed a few insects. No thank you, I do not eat bugs! John feeds me much better. How else could I weigh almost thirty pounds? Handsome cat I am, with all muscle and glistening Asian gray fur complete with worldwide modesty. John uses me—he has never told anyone, but I know—as a guard cat. Once he was thinking about going somewhere, and then he thought, *Why worry? I have a twenty-pound panther for a guard.* He is right. I will do anything to keep him safe. Mainly, I try to keep him in upscale restaurants where they are playing football games, and the people in the restaurant love me. They bring me food "on the side." For that matter, they bring John food on the side, since he loves to eat appetizers. If you are wondering about how he brings me everywhere, it is because John has concocted a "very tasteful" cat pajama that says "Service Cat." If forced, I will emit one cute "Meow" and then just stare at whomever with my beautiful eyes that have never told a lie, and that really gets to them. (No such thing as a lie in the cat dictionary. Doesn't exist in our vocabulary. Of course, I have a totally different understanding of what a lie is, and if need be, I can do an excellent job, especially when wearing my silk service cat pajamas. Boy, do I look hot!)

Hmmm, I wonder how I can parley my beautifulness into having John do more things for me? Then again, even I have to be careful. Once or twice John was thinking of dragging me to Hollywood and trying to get me some kind of a cat part in the movies. "We" looked into it a bit, and it was not for me. Mainly because John was using— yes, I said "using"—me to meet whomever. Like I said, sometimes I have to keep an eye on that guy. Not too tough, however, and I guess that guy could use a date once in a while.

Time to hit the road! John fed me just what I ordered and washed my paws with hydrogen peroxide and a few other spots that he thought needed a cleanup. (Hope he doesn't overdo it and put some bleach spots on my beautiful fur. Like I always meow, he needs watching.) We are going to San Diego today, as I instructed his subconscious while he was reading the sports section. He was reading the surfing section, and he thinks that is where he got the idea. Just before he hit the ignition and got the car going, he looked at me, straight in my cat eyes, smiled, and said, "Casey, you are a piece of work!" Hmmm...makes me wonder about that guy sometimes.

Money in Big Sur

*W*hat do you want, dear reader? Did you answer right away, did you give it a couple of seconds of thought, or are you still thinking about it? Most would blurt out, "I want a million dollars!" With more thought they would blurt out, "Oh, heck, I better have a billion." Maybe they wouldn't say a thing for quite a while. Maybe their first thought would be, *Wait a minute, I heard somewhere that money can't fix everything*. Then they would have more confusing thoughts, more consternations, how about this, and how about that, and what ifs. They realize that money can't fix everything. It could be that the person, when asked "What do you want?" has a myriad of problems. Where would they begin?

There was a very popular TV show put out some time ago. I think you can still see it around on TV. The half-hour show was *The Millionaire*. The basis of the show was that a person would be given a million dollars. Simple, that's all. In every show, time after time, the person with the million dollars went bonkers. It made them think too much is my best guess.

Okay, let's play with you right now. Here is a billion dollars. Now what? Where would you begin?

First I would put the money in a bank.

Then what?

Then I would think of what to do with it.

Then what?

Duhhhhhhh. Have to think it over.

We're presuming all this time you have a "normal" human body, and you can function by yourself, carry on your daily duties, that you are self-contained with maybe a couple years of college. I see where I am having trouble here defining what a normal person is. We will just have to imagine you are a physically and mentally normal person. (Unlike us cats; we are all not normal in that we are all great!) So, normal person, after somehow putting your money in places where they will not take it away from you, decide to go on a trip around the world. Should be fun because you've never been out of Indiana. Whoopee! Oops, you had to tell all your closest buddies and relations what happened to you since you couldn't possibly keep this all to yourself. Of course, some cat touches here and there were made, and what the heck, you gave in. Lucky you made plans to go around the world, because your phone was ringing off the hook by people who, face it, wanted your money. Learned one lesson in a hurry. "Keep my mouth shut!"

Your trip begins. Airplane ride after airplane ride from one country to the next, having nasty people to deal with wherever you go. You have hardly ever traveled before and had no idea they had piranha-like people in charge of these traveling trips. Lesson two. "Traveling is a bitch." You then hire some type of a good man or woman, Friday or Tuesday, or whatever humans call them. (We cats just call them with a meow.) They are to plan everything for you so you can just enjoy yourself and not have to worry about ONE thing. After six months, you realize they have been absconding with the money, and you have them jailed for a long time. Lesson three. "Lawyers are expensive."

Time for travel to Big Sur in Northern California. Have to go and get some real thinking done and find out what you can do with a billion dollars. Ridiculous, it seems, but so far after about two months you have gotten into more trouble and hassles than you have ever gotten into before in your entire life. Big Sur is great! Just remember number one rule. Keep your mouth shut, but open it a little. At least say you have a great pension plan for a long time. It's all in the hands of your lawyers. Now, you just want to be healthy and happy. Whew, you finally made a step where you are somewhat relaxed. No one is trying to steal your money, and you are not getting bitched out by morons constantly. Every day you sit in a tub of water overlooking the Pacific Ocean and go to some classes that are supposed to help your overall being, and it all seems pretty good. Wine, good food, and other "stuff" is around, and you give it a try from time to time. Meanwhile, you can't help but meet other people who are there as well. After some time, you realize that so many are just "tubbing it" and getting bombed. What? You wonder if there is a rule for this.

After checking out of Big Sur, it is time to go to San Francisco, right up the road. You have a nice car, and now you have figured out some safeguards as to how to guard your money. Seems complicated for what was supposed to be a walk on the beach, but, oh well, it still is pretty good. You now carry your money around in the trunk of your car in twenty-dollar bills in about six duffle bags, about $100,000 altogether. You figure, and since you have never figured higher than five thousand dollars at a time, this seems like pretty good backup money to you. You make it to San Francisco and check into the best place you can find. Looks good. Now what? All this dough and nowhere to go. (Reminds me of a song I heard back home?) You wonder if this is the twilight zone—different but just the same. Maybe you need a pet. All the hot tubbers at Big Sur really "dig" pets.

Down to the SPCA to take a look at the pets. Kind of hot in here, so you take off your coat and look around. I just happened to lay the coat down next to the newly born kittens area. One mother cat had eleven kittens. All those little animals sure jerk at your heart, and maybe tomorrow you will donate a bunch and help this place out. Yes, that is exactly what you will do! Finally an idea of worth and yee haw, now you will help something! Don't know why it makes you feel good, but it does. Back home when doing chores twice a day for fifteen years, no animal ever tugged at your heart. Just your dear mother tugging on your toe, telling you it is time for chores.

Put my coat on and decided to go to a place to have a drink and a bite to eat. I ordered a drink and went in my pocket to get some money. Surprise! Both my wallet and a small kitten popped out. He was only three days old, but I could tell he was trying to tell me something. Uh, okay. We went to the bathroom, and then headed back home. He went right to sleep and didn't make a meow, kept my side warm and guarded my money, I imagined. On the way home I noticed it was as though someone was talking to me with no noise. After a while, I realized it was no noise; it was someone talking directly into my mind. In addition, I was talking back to them. Seemed right in line with the rest of the baloney I had been getting since having a billion dollars. After more discussion with this voice, I realized it was the kitten. He told me how old he was and that he, too, had just learned that he had this incredible skill of being able to mentally therapize and lots more. Right now he wanted to go to bed, and he told me to buy a six-pack so I could relax and watch the game. He said it would take a while for me to figure this out, but it would be the best thing he ever did. I knew. I can see the future as well.

This is the incredible story of how John and I began. When he laid his coat down by our cage, my abilities told me this was the lucky guy. And I mean he was the lucky guy. Maybe I should have waited around for someone else. Kidding aside, where else could I find a guy with a billion dollars who trusted a cat to manage it? At three days old to boot? Mew! Mew!

To Sleep Over or Not

*L*ast night I was a very busy cat. John had been sleeping for a couple of hours, and I was walking around the house and listening to the radio, which is so boring, even for a cat. I decided to take a look inside John's mind and find out how he was doing. (I almost don't need to do it since I can read from body posturing, noises, and hundreds of other outside indications what a person is thinking, what they are like, and well, you name it. With this mink coat I wear all the time and what I have in and around my entire body, what more can you expect? Not too much humility for sure and a great sense of humor. See, I told you.)

For the best mind-reading possible, I have to place my whiskers somewhere on the person's body. I don't have to at all, but it is like watching and listening to your own home hundred-foot movie screen and somebody is bringing you popcorn or scotch. This was even better since John was asleep. I placed one of my whiskers in his ear. He was thinking entirely too much. All jumbled up and worried and guessing and hopping from one dream to another, and he was going backward as fast as possible into a nowhere area. I cured that immediately. I just flipped a whisker inside the ear, and then it all went to a day at the beach without problems, a beautiful view of the ocean with a pleasant breeze, and a smile on his face for no reason at all.

John has to do a more efficient job of dreaming like I do. I am never asleep, as I am constantly aware of what is going on in my mind, with my other mind (explain later...maybe), and I know what is going on all around me that goes into the cosmos. (Don't wish you could? The cosmos can be very boring, like there are miles and miles of nothing in most continents, and so it is with the cosmos. Boring at a glance and even to explore further will only bore you more.) Of course, I do it all naturally, and yet I have even improved on my cat-given abilities and continue to do so every day. The only thing I want is a Bentley with John driving, of course, but it is not a huge want, and since I can get it whenever I want, I tend to do other things that could be more challenging. The way to make one's dreaming into fact in one's life is to make a plan for what you want to do and accomplish. How you do it is the key. John has me. Since there are not many of me around, one has to do the best they can by whatever means they stumble upon. Anything could work. The billionaire in Mexico listens to numbers talk to him. The devices and methods used by people to accomplish a more productive and happy life are almost as many as there are people. Now, I must leave you hanging and guessing what the exact methods are. There are millions. You could always buy me, and that would cost a lot, and then I would leave when I wanted to, or leave you in a closet somewhere with your brain rattled because you tried to treat me wrongly. (Nobody has ever treated me wrongly. I know what they are thinking, so I treat them in a way they were thinking of treating me. Sometimes it isn't too good for them, but hey, what's a cat to do?)

The only surefire way to achieve what you want in about ten seconds is to have me, and hope I may want to help you. But I am still a cat, and to date no one has ever predicted what a cat will do. So far I have been with John for all of my knowledgeable life. This was three seconds after I was born, and John took me home, and I "guided" him as to what to do to help me out. Now, I am about three years old and still laughing at John's jokes. That seems to be all I want, and you know what? I should "suggest" to John to get a Bentley. Just thinking of what he would say might make me laugh out loud, and then he would think I was ill and attempt to "cure" me. That would make me laugh even more, and the thought of it all right now is too much. That's why I won't "get" John a Bentley yet. I will have to prepare for so much laughter that it could hurt. Hmmm, I could program him not to make Bentley jokes, but I would never do anything to interrupt his "flow." Oops there I go, laughing out loud again, meowing and jumping around and waving my tail and acting ridiculous. Can't let anybody see me doing this. But I have learned greatly from this, and have learned that even I have limitations. Only one, don't get John a Bentley just yet. There must be something about the British and their automobiles. I dare not think any further about this matter right now. Back to the cosmos, which is so much easier.

Physical Fitness

I'm a cat. Physical fitness, why? I stretch and jump on and off everything in the house, and I only eat when and what I want to eat. I get a kick out of John getting up at 4:30 a.m. every day, mumbling and cussing and taking aspirin so he can do his crazy exercises. Don't get me wrong, because I enjoy it very much. Watching him stumble and bumble around the house so early in the morning is very entertaining. Truly, enough to make me laugh. However, he never quits. Up and down and all around, drinking water and counting out loud and huffing and puffing and cussing every now and then. Quite a show that is, making those muscles grow! One day he was so exhausted that while taking a shower afterward, he fell out of the tub. Shower curtains, soap, and water and John on the floor. I was concerned, so I went into the bathroom immediately, and there he was, lying on the floor with the shower curtains wrapped around him. He grabbed the commode and slowly got up and was content, and then he gave me a pet and laughed out loud because he thought he could have been killed, but he was okay. Humans can't figure it out. Be like me, I say! I know it's impossible for them to do so, but I am training John as fast as he will let me. Yesterday, I saw him staring out the window with his face between the venetian blinds just like I do. I looked at him, and he looked at me and smiled. Like I said, I've got to keep a close eye on that guy.

Cuba

*N*o matter where I go, everybody wants more money. The word *money* does not exist in cat language. I decided to take a look into the world of money, and please let me tell you what I discovered. It just so happened that my whiskers brushed gently against John's head when we were getting ready for a trip, and it was as though a gigantic neon sign kept blinking on and off…money, money, money! We got in the car and turned on the radio, and more money ads or people talking about money kept popping up. Even, I must add, a story about a cat that inherited fifty million dollars after his owner passed away. So, I reasoned, if a cat is involved, it must be good, and who knows, maybe I can get John a few million so I won't be reading those money blinking messages his mind is continually emitting.

Time for further research, I concluded. So I did some quick reading in the papers. Read a few books by Warren Buffett and Bill Gates, and I was ready. Oh, I also checked out how much cats make in Hollywood, since John is always trying to send me there, and find out how much they make. One cat got almost a million dollars, so I decided to call good ole Uncle Al and make some money. We met at our favorite place, a warm chimney high above the blue and windy sea overlooking all of San Francisco at midnight. It was cozy and one of the most beautiful views in the whole world, and such a fantastic smell enveloped our cat senses. Al said he got a new kind of cigar that didn't bother his whiskers or stink up his mink coat. Al said it cost about $80 a cigar, and they were lying all over the place at Chez

Paree. The one he had was "found" in the crux of a tree, hopefully to be reunited with its owner, after a great meal of whatever people eat. We began to speak about the cigar business and wondered how much it made and went over all the particulars. We decided it was at least a billion-dollar business coming out of Havana alone. The next logical question was how could we do what the Cubans do? Al immediately started humming some rumba tune, dancing around the chimney, and waving his hat to and fro like Ricky Nelson did. The plan began. All we had to do was go to Cuba, get an ocean liner full of cigars, sail it to Miami, and sell them back here. Meow!

We "booked" a trip to Cuba and were there the next day. Our brethren were legion, and we got all the info we needed in ten minutes, including all the greatest cigars in the world that we could carry. The plan was simple. Send an order to the cigar factory for the absolute best cigars in the world to be shipped to Miami as soon as possible. (It was a rush job, we said, and that Roi-tan was in competition so we wanted the best price as well.) All was well, and two billion of the cigars were loaded on the boat and ready to go, except for the "filthy lucre." Payment was due tomorrow after the ship had been loaded, and as soon as the money arrived, it was anchors away. I mentioned the *anchors away* description of departure to Al, and he immediately began a marine march using a cigar for an M-1 rifle, singing "Anchors Away, Me Boy," and showing with the beat his shiny teeth on every tenth note.

At the time of Al's anchors away march and showing off his gleaming teeth, we were "relaxing" in one of Cuba's best and most famous bistros, and high above us was a balcony that went around the entire restaurant. I noticed two of our brethren paying close attention to Al and me, and they indicated for us to join them. We did, and they were beautiful, wonderful, informative hosts. We told them what we were doing, and they told us it so happened they knew exactly where Castro lived, and would we like to go there? Ahem, of course, we said; if it would not inconvenience anyone, we would be more than delighted, and would they like to come to Miami? Immediate smiles and purrs and synchronized tail weaving and waving began to blend in with the beautiful Cuban music being played in the restaurant below. After "taking" a taxi, we were in Castro's villa and were shown everywhere, lots of places that only a cat would know about. Voila! In no time, we were in Castro's study, perusing his monetary records, and we found that he had huge accounts in Switzerland and, you guessed it, New York... Ahem again! Castro accepted his cigar payments on his personal iPod, where he was assured the money was accepted, and he replied with his secret star of approval. We were able to secure both sending and accepting codes in the blink of my eye. They were kept in the very bottom of Castro's personal whiskey drinking glass. He kept the numbers there because he loved to drink, and he loved to see how much money he had as often as possible. The rest was a cat's meow. We showed money transfers on the bottom of his whiskey glass, and the cigars were ours. Why stop there? Make enough to make a cat laugh, you say? I also transferred all the money in all of his accounts to John. As to not let the old boy down, we also changed the numbers on the bottom of Castro's whiskey glass, and put some extra "catnip" in his whiskey supply to help him sleep until all was kosher. Well, kind of. If that isn't enough money for John, please let me know.

As the cat vine goes, Putin also has quite a lot of Russian overboots or whatever they use for money. His favorite beverage is you know what. Our beautiful hosts also knew friends in the Kremlin. They didn't demand a large fee, but I hope Al doesn't run out of catnip real soon or forget the words to "Anchors Away." You know female cats, beautiful but so demanding! Meow, I'm getting out of here!

Music and Cats Confused

C ats are kind of confused by music. As if we are confused by anything at all is pretty hard to say. Since I am a different cat (really), I have to tell you what I think about the music I hear. Horrible, just horrible! Most of it anyhow, but today I heard a song that made me pat my paws on John's dash and emit a small meow his way. (John laughed and gave my cheek a squeeze.) The name of the song is "Orange-Colored Sky" by Milton DeLugg. I was going to guess at first it was Cole Porter, but I wasn't far off. Nat King Cole brought it into prominence, and it is simply beautiful. "Crash, bam, alakazam, on an orange-colored sky." Those words would make a cat proud, with such originality and all the absolute rest of it. Music is delightful to my soul, and I have already implanted a thought to John to get a recording so that I can listen to it whenever I want. (Pretty much sums me up, "Whenever I want.") The song and the words are so absolutely, fantastically beautiful that I had to write about it. It opened up more of the world for me. It had more beauty, more sound, more cleverness, and it was all put together in a couple of minutes. I do hear beautiful music, I mean the kind that is on the radio and such, all the time. I also hear great music of my surroundings, but most of the music I hear (and such) is enough to make a cat laugh. So funny!

During the Super Bowl, I took a moment at half time to watch the show. (John took me for a ride so he wouldn't get too excited, and I missed some of it.) The music I heard must sound like the music humans hear at night when cats decide to sing to the moon, to each other, or just humming, screaming along if you want. Horrible! Horrible! I know the artistic world says all is music, all is art, and all is poetry, and to answer those statements, I will refer you to Uncle Al. Being careful, most of the stuff I hear is not even junk, but when they get it right, it makes me very happy.

I had a discussion about this with Uncle Al, and he was mystified. He kept himself busy by catching flies and falling asleep and giving me the "I am so bored, and when can we ride a few pigeons down to the market and get some fish" look. Got to love Uncle Al in some ways, and in other ways, you would think he communes with the devil. Because I think the devil would not know what to do, and let's get real—the devil has more to do than converse about riding pigeons or where the best batch of stinko fish can be found. Moving on.

Music is going through a down curve much like stock and bonds do. Nowadays, you can buy it for a penny on the dollar, just a bunch of people hollering, yelling, making noises and faces, and beating on stuff, sometimes each other. (I was observing some kittens at play when that music came within their hearing, and they ran the other way. So cute. I took a brief glance into their minds, and one kitten expressed it best, "Let's get out of here!" So succinct and cat like.)

John is thinking about taking me for a ride, so I will nudge him toward a record store, and we'll see what we shall see. I like Sinatra as well, and so does John, so I think I have a pretty good chance of getting some great music. Mealtimes I will hang out with the kittens, and hear what they have to say about what they are seeing in this world. If one of them starts to talk about riding pigeons, I will dissuade him as soon as possible. Cats with manners simply don't ride pigeons. Seagulls are okay, but pigeons are so chancy, and forget sparrows completely. Why I remember the time, Pa…

Cat's Pajamas

I find John to be pretty funny. Today, while he was talking to me, he said he was an easy touch. He said, "Touch me, it's easy." I had to meow out loud, it was so funny. Hence, the term "'nuff to make a cat laugh!" "Awctually" all the cat jokes and references one hears throughout time are spot-on. We cats have been around— civilized cats, I mean—for about 10,000 years, and please forget my thousand-pound cousins. But keep an eye out. They are almost as good-looking as I am, but to be most succinct, they will eat you if they feel like it. I won't go near one even at the zoo. If they want- ed, they could scale those walls in a second. I know. I have heard them thinking while at the zoo with John, and all that goes through their thousand-pound cat brains is *when is feeding time, let's eat the zookeeper, let's jump the wall,* or *let's eat anything that moves in the enclosure.* Remember, they are not nice at all. Like a beauti- ful Siamese cat I knew for a short time, and she was so like me, beautiful, with mink pajamas, a Chinese smile, a mellow meow, and such a charming way about her. She could not read minds like me, however. I knew her for a short time, and the things she was and was not thinking were simply abhorrent to me. Her mind was bits and fragments of desires for food, sleep, warmth, and even a bath from a cat doctor. Ha! I should have had John give her a bath and see how she liked that! John uses Ivory soap on me and sings some kind of Sinatra song that drives me nuts. If he would sing "The Star- Spangled Banner" and take the part of Kate Smith, I would be much more manageable. Actually, I am quite manageable, but I have to keep up some sort of a cat demeanor.

After several weeks of seeing her on the neighbor's roof, I quit going to that roof. I guess John's mind has spoiled me. Only because slowly, but surely, I am getting him to think more and more like a cat. Every now and then, he winks at me and gives me a mysterious smile, and at those times, it is hard to read his mind or to get a whisker on him. When he is asleep, reading his mind is like an MGM Grand production night. If I don't like what he is dreaming about, I meow and stick my tail in his ear and change the channel. No doubt about it, John is a full-time job. If I can get him to start using a different type of bath soap, I am sure I will have made him perfect. I only need ask, "Do you get room and board, love, movies every night, car rides, and someone to bathe you for free?" As the noted saying goes throughout history and when something is perfect and beautiful, it's the cat's pajamas. I rest my case.

Cuban Cigars

*A*l and I met at our usual meeting place, a warm chimney high above San Francisco with a 360-degree view of the bridges, the bay, the ballpark, and all of the buildings in the city proper. San Francisco is small by most city standards throughout the world, eight hundred thousand in population in only sixty-four square miles. Al and I like it here. We have seagull service at all times. And it was unknown to all except me that on this exact spot and height was the perfect place for the embryo of the greatest ideas and plans the world has ever known. Tonight was the time to put all our ideas and plans together and create what would soon be the greatest achievement ever accomplished by mankind, and it would be done by one cat, me! I have no ego, but I like to accomplish great things, and that is why Al was here. Somehow, some way, he activates all my senses and brings them into complete alignment with all the powers and worlds that are now, have been, and will be. That's a lot!

Al was thoroughly enjoying the best cigar the world has known. Sitting there beside the chimney, we were totally enveloped in a blue-gray cloud that fit in perfectly under the light of a full moon. The slight breeze coming off the ocean "on a clear and windy sea" gave me exactly what I needed to begin the greatest accomplishment of all time, invisibility at will by all living creatures! I told Al, and he said, "We're already invisible. Nobody can see us now."

I said, "But only if we stay here, and we cannot duplicate these conditions all the time."

Al said, "Why not? All you need is a cigar and a match, and poof, nobody can see you. You can even make clouds and leave them about in case people think, *Where there is a cloud, there is a person.* Besides after the "deal" with Castro, we have just bought two billion dollars' worth of Havana cigars with Castro's money. The more cigars we sell, the better. If we can ship all over the world, and everyone smokes more Havana cigars, the planet will be in an aromatic fog such that the entire planet will be invisible. Maybe even the aliens won't be able to kidnap us like they say they do on the Art Bell Show. In fact, the silly aliens will probably buy ship-loads of cigars from us, and soon the entire cosmos will be one giant Havana cigar smokescreen that smells like the dancing girls we met in Cuba. Boy, could they dance."

After a dance or two and a cigar, all were happier. Our science laboratory had also discovered that by mixing cigars, catnip, and the sweet smell of cute Cuban dancing girls, we had completely knocked out any cancerous cells that had been associated with ci-gars. In addition, while smoking these "special" cigars, every other kind of cancer known to mankind was eradicated as well. Our fan-tastic byproduct, as is so often the case of great inventions, saved the entire world from cancer forevermore. It was thought that the sweet smell of the cute Cuban dancers was the main ingredient. (Needless to say, scientists all over the world are investigating the cancer killer in the cute Cuban dancers' sweet body sweat.) Now, for the aliens!

This Whole Football Betting Thing

This whole football betting thing was a high-tech masterpiece. The betters could bet on anything they wanted, even before the odds were placed, with no way of knowing if what they had betted on had already expired, and the betting line could choose to let them win or lose, whatever they wanted. Sounds like something my Uncle Al would do, er, wanted to do. Besides, we're talking about cats betting using sardines in "receptacles" behind fashionable restaurants in the great city of San Francisco. (Maybe if they read this, they will get smart. Would you believe just donate the sardines to the SPCA center? Back to the high-tech holdup. We contacted some of the people in MIT who had been out gambling with gamblers for a couple of years, and asked them, "Do you have any suggestions as to what to do?" Considering some of them had been kept in cages without any evidence for a couple of weeks naked, cold, and starving, for simply winning at a card game because they had more brains, didn't seem fair. I mean, it's okay to think when you are gambling, isn't it? They were so happy. They gathered all the evidence, completely legally, of course. Got all the people together, wherever, who had rigged the sporting bets, and contacted them. Nobody but those who were there knew what happened. Use your imagination, just a little bit.

The *San Francisco Chronicle's* sports section said there was a fresh wind in sports about people gambling on games. Although it had been going on since the days of the coliseum, it would now take a respite. If they only knew the whole gambling fiasco was brought about by a bitch who wanted to pour Stoli on John's head, almost causing a cat to have to walk thirty miles home and being completely grouchy all the while. Oops, I forgot about Seagull Joe, but it was game day, and I knew he would be gambling. I could not get a hold of him. All was forgiven when I saw Joe Montana and Will Clark having a couple of laughs over by the water cooler. Talk about cool cats!

It was a big football game in the Bay Area. San Francisco was favored by six. I dared not, well almost, use my mental abilities to know what exactly the score would be. John and I had been invited to a guest box that was so comfortable, I was thinking of moving here. We had whatever the best of what there was to offer. There were giant screens all over to show the game. There were hostesses bringing you everything you wanted. I have to say, it was the cat's meow! One particular small screen off to the side had numbers and football games being bounced on the screen continually. More people seemed to be watching the small screen than the football game. Hmmm, I found out it gave a continual update as to what the score was of the games, and how they stacked up with the betting numbers, the odds given them, and the bets placed on them. This was much more than eighth-grade math, and the implications behind each odd given and the bet made could be quite great. My whiskers twitched. I blinked mysteriously. The game was afoot. The betting world today is not just about the score of the game. It can include bets and odds placed on anything from analgesics to Zimbabwe. You think it up, and a bet can be placed on it. It's your money. Well, it's theirs, as well, but the average better is knocking heads with some people who, yes, I will say it again, knock heads.

Not too long ago, a bunch of very smart students from MIT took on the gambling industry and its various types of illegal cousins literally all around the world. They picked and chose carefully, and they went in teams to gamble and made significant amounts of money, like millions and millions. Their IQs could not be measured, nor could their grasp of what all of "us" know. Putting all that money in suitcases was too tedious for them. After packing the money and lugging it all home, they would sometimes leave a trail of dough falling out of the suitcases they had sloppily packed. Upon arriving in his frat house, someone told of the trail of fifty-dollars bills leading up to the fraternity. Okay, already. They got bigger suitcases. It took a couple of years, but finally, casinos all over the world had an MO on them, and it was getting tougher and tougher for them to make a couple of million dollars a weekend. They were eventually banned from every casino in the world, and that is the end of that story. They were threatened physically, scared, and imprisoned in some countries, and they finally said, "Nuts, this is not fun anymore." Casinos and the powers that be are exactly that, power, plenty of brains, not real good brains, but lots of them. They are devious, lethal, and deadly if they have to be. Outside of the good old USA, you better be real careful; even here it helps to be very aware. As I was looking at the betting screen and the people around me on that seemingly wonderful, breezy, tree leaf falling Sunday afternoon in October, I sensed there was also great danger lurking. I knew it, I had seen enough, and I had to get John out of there.

Good old boy that he was, he was as happy as my parents when they had us eleven kittens. Probably happier than my dad, for sure. He had it all. Great chair, great screen, food and drink of any kind, wanted to bet (almost got you), and pretty girls would bring whatever was wanted to him immediately. John liked "immediately" most of all. His motto should have been "Just bring it!" The servers had figured him out, and every nine minutes, they would go over and fill up the guy with the cat in the backpack. "He tips us five dollars when one of these drinks alone costs twenty!" "I'd pour one on his head," one little bitch said, "but that cat is kind of big, and once I could have sworn, I heard him growl. But when I looked, he was smiling sweet as can be." Between me wanting to bite off the arm of a bitch because she was going to dump a drink on John, and some of the "hosts", bent noses and all, closing in on John, I persuaded him to leave right away.

As we were leaving the stadium in Santa Clara on that beautiful day, John said out loud, "Whatta racket!" He, too, had noticed the betting screen, the odds, the bets, the room beginning to fill up with ne'er-do-wells, and the complete sleaziness behind a glitzy curtain of success, drinks and food, and lots of ways to make easy money. He looked at me in the rearview mirror and laughed and gave me a knowing nod. Time for me to go to work.

We met in our usual meeting place by the chimney on top of the roof of one of the energy power points in the vast cosmos. Three-sixty-degree view of San Francisco on a beautiful starry night, slight sea wind, the smell of the chimney smoke, and some of my cronies, two being Uncle Al and Seagull Joe. We were going to get to the bottom or top of some football gambling shenanigans going on all over the planet. Wanna bet?! I probably wouldn't have given it a thought, what with caveat emptor and all, but when that stupid bitch was going to go off on John, that did it! John would have reacted, and then what? How would I get home? I can't drive a car. Yet.

Australia

*J*ohn had to take me to the cat doctor. I was causing problems around the house, and I would leave so as not to make a mess. I could not live outside all the time, because let's face it, I am spoiled. John understood, and we made the somber trip to the cat doctor. The vet had no diagnosis available, and as Elvis said, "Return to sender. Go home." At home I was sniffling and acting, well, like a sick cat. John said, "Maybe a trip will help you. Maybe there is something in the air that is making you ill." I sniffed, rolled over, and waved my paws around in the air. "That's enough," John said. "We are going to Australia."

As usual we sat in the front of the plane, and I wore my orange cat care jacket with pills for John. John was a bit under the weather as well, and we made a heckuva team. I felt like taking some of his pills, but I thought it might kill me, and then what would John do? Everyone was so nice to me as I was having cat dreams, waving my paws and tail around. I think I heard John laughing through my dream catnap. We landed in the middle of the night, staggered off to our lodging, and slept the sleep of the sick and hopeless. We had a good night's sleep, in other words.

In the morning we went out to see what we could see. I was in the backpack, and I just lay back and looked at the sky. I noticed I could breathe better, however, and even John acted more chipper. (He wanted to get his Irish hands on some Australian beer, I knew.)

We soon found a place that served food and drink and in we went. They were all speaking so fast and garbled that I just went to mind-reading and after a while, I shut it all down. John had found some Australian beer, and he was telling all about the cat in the bag. They thought I was a little roo. He made some off-color joke that rhymed with roo, and I almost got sick again.

By the end of the day I felt normal. Whisker, eyes, tail, nails, tongue and ears were all 100 percent. John was about 22 percent. That was the alcoholic content of the beer he had been drinking all day, and now he said he was pooped, which describes himself and fits his condition exactly. Back to the hotel and to sleep, I thought. We had to pass through a lounge where all were imbibing and carry-ing on, and they noticed me in the backpack. More roo talk ensued, and now John let it all go and said I was a miniature Bengalese tiger, perfect pet, never did that or this, and a real treasure. All were impressed, and we were asked to join them. The conversation got around to the big story "Down Under." Seems there was a bunch of super, maybe souped-up, kangaroos going around the country caus-ing lots of trouble, and something had to be done. They laughed and said, "If the tiger in the backpack would ever awake, he might be able to help us out here." Raucous laughter ensued. John said, "You have big cats over here. Why don't you get them to help out?" Even more laughter from the Aussie mates, and they said, "Honky donkey, wonky blonky, and fiddle biddle, black jack. What? How's about a snort, old sport?" John laughed politely, bought a round, and we went off to our lodging. John went off to a 22 percent sauce sleep, while by now I was feeling as good as ever. I felt a plan of ac-tion beginning to take place. If for nothing else, it might help them quit speaking that honky, bonky, wonky lingo. All that gibberish was hilarious actually, and I immediately pulled a pillow over my head and laughed myself to sleep. Indeed, 'nuff to make a cat laugh!

The next day I met some of Seagull Joe's friends, and we spoke about the kangaroos. They said that until just a few years ago, all was normal and then, all of a sudden, there were these giant roos running all over the country causing problems, injuring people and animals. Coincidentally, a few years ago there was talk of UFOs being spotted. Nobody paid much attention, what with 22 percent beer being served all over the place, not to mention the backup vodka. Talk about the roos causing trouble. I said maybe it would pay to take a look, and could I get a "taxi" ride to where the kangaroos hung out. (Or, whatever roos do.) "Sure," one big seagull said. "My name is Sammy, and I would be glad to help. I have never given cats rides before, but it sounds like I should give it a go. Hop on, and let's see how it works." I did, and off we flew. This way and that way at first, but shortly we were flying right along headed to where the roos were. They were in a small gully about five miles outside of town, and since we were in the air, nobody paid any attention. I asked Sammy to go low so I could take a closer look, and he did. We actually landed in a tree where they were busily eating leaves, and I was able to get excellent readings. Most of them had typical kangaroo thoughts like, *Where was I? Where am I? I am hungry. I feel good*, and of course, *Let's go out and just jump around!* A couple of the bigger ones had no thoughts at all; their minds were simply vacant. Some were twice as big as the regular roos and were very aggressive for no reason at all apparently. One spotted us and, with a mighty jump, came at us completely unexpected. Like a veteran taxi cab driver, Sammy flew off, and then gave him a caw or two. I just held on and knew what I had to do.

It had been some time since I contacted the aliens. We had had a misunderstanding, which was quickly cleared up, and we now had a workable relationship. I told them what was happening, and did they know anything about giant kangaroos with no brains that could jump over a barn and carry a person in their pouch? Their attitude was considerably hostile without fear. They were extremely dangerous, and if unchecked, could wreak havoc over all of Australia. (Maybe they would mess up their 22 percent stuff and then things might really get serious....just had to kid the Down Under men.) The aliens soon sent me an answer by mental telepathy, of course. It seems a group of their kind had performed experiments on the kangaroos, which were not permitted. That group had been dealt with in their own legal system, and there would be no more of that experimentation. I said, "How can we control this problem? They have no minds, they don't understand a thing, and it is impossible to communicate with them, unless it is death." My harsh evaluation, but I was completely correct. We had to come up with a solution before all of Australia was overrun with these mindless, mean roos, smashing whatever and whomever they came upon.

I contacted Uncle Al telepathically, as he was sitting at our meeting place, the chimney, with some of his friends. He immediately said it would be no problem, and here was the solution. "Gather all the roos with no brains, big tails and legs, huge muscles, and steel piston-like arms, and show them how a game of football is played. What they see they will do. Dress them up just like the football players. Place huge vats of 22 percent stuff in their locker rooms. Also, introduce the Coco Cabana Cha Cha Cha Cancer Curing Cigars. We will make a short movie of a super kangaroo smoking one, and that should do the trick."

Uncle Al was correct. We followed the plan and went one step further. We even built a giant stadium in the outback where the aboriginal people live to give them entertainment. It was a smashing success. Complete imitation of the professional American football game was put in place. We had the big kangaroos completely focused on playing football, drinking 22 percent stuff, and puffing cigars. A couple of them had somehow learned to communicate, and they wanted to be sports announcers since they had hurt their tails. Some aboriginals became the roos' agents. They got all of them tremendous contracts, as well as themselves, and made tons of money. Too much success is exactly that. Many football players, announcers, and lawyers, ahem, are going to Australia "for the waters" they say. (Remember the movie *Casablanca*?) Maybe the Nazis will be next. Bring back Bogart and Bergman and the rest of the cast. We may at least get a good movie out of this. Whatever it takes, and apparently it takes a lot to make a good movie. WWII and now giant brainless kangaroos—sounds perfect for a typical Hollywood movie. We slept the sleep of an ancient mariner's dream whose ship was in bad seas.

Mother Goose

$\mathcal{M}$ other Goose said it best: "The cow jumped over the moon, and the cat ran away with the spoon." I understand it completely. But I have an upper paw on you because I am a cat. Not only that, but I have the greatest mind that was never possible to conceive. It's delightful. I really do know it all, and listening to John trying to get an insurance policy makes me take some extra catnip before we have our chimney midnight meeting. Whenever we decide—"we" being Seagull Joe, Uncle Al, and his protégés— to have a meeting, it can be of great importance or just otherwise. Tonight was otherwise, and the protégés of Uncle Al were getting restless. They had heard of all kinds of things going on, and why weren't we doing something about it? "Okay, pray tell what might this trouble you conceive to be?" I said. Lots of meowing and a few of the up-comers starting cat-batting the air, and I said, "Okay, get up on the chimney and tell us what you want to say." I put everyone present on mind-meld, and this is what one of the protégés said in so many meows.

Within about twenty miles south from where we were sitting was the atom-busting linear accelerator of the world. (This world, anyhow, as you know it, dear reader.) He said his friends from that area were finding it impossible to get their usual great meal that they had enjoyed for many years. Kiddingly, they referred to it as pheasant under bush. (Well, at least they had been to a fashionable restaurant dump somewhere.) He also said some of his best buddies were missing. He even thought, though being a rookie, that he sensed a hint of evil near the accelerator. Another rookie piped up and said, "Whoever hangs around that atom cruncher is asking for trouble. They're just looking for an easy meal and a ride to the moon, albeit in scattered parts. Come to San Fran and get a decent sardine meal. I met some of those guys once, and they were all hippied out. They just don't want to work." (Hummm, I have heard this in other places. You don't think?)

Cat glances were exchanged, and I said, "This is how our meetings and discussions should be. Speak one's mind and everyone listen. We are perfect gentlemen or trying to be, and proper communication is of utmost importance. Giving each other cat looks and pulling tails is not the way to communicate. Now you know, and if it happens again, we'll throw you down the chimney, or worse."

One rookie said, "Guttercat should know." (He is the one who rolled down the roof and, if not for the gutter, would have had a long fall.) Laughter and cat-batting all around, and once again, humor can bring about a tremendous closeness and understanding. I said, "Okay, let's get some paws on the ground there, and if our great friend and flyer and some of his men would cooperate, we can put about twenty cats on the ground in twenty minutes."

The rookies loved the idea, and twenty were chosen, and away they went. The others who wanted to go could go after them in a short while. Such camaraderie was great to see and feel. Love those cigars we were all smoking and the attitude of these young cats. Guttercat was going on the first landing. Some cat smiles indicated and hoped Guttercat would not start laughing at the fifteen-mile accelerator. He was smoking a cigar as he took off on the back of Seagull Joe, against regulations, and he probably thought the accelerator was a gas pedal on a car. Tremendous cat, so enthusiastic, but sometimes he leaped before he should have put his cigar down. What's new? Who hasn't? "Meow!"

Next day, Seagull Joe and Guttercat returned. Joe was all right, but Guttercat had some nasty radiation burns. It seemed he saw a pheasant, and in trying to get a bite to eat to help him carry on, he fell in a huge hole, like as big a hole as one needs to launch a warhead. Seagull Joe risked his life going into the hole and getting Guttercat out. Guttercat had grown up real quick. He told me what he found, and promptly, another chimney meeting was scheduled for midnight of that same night. Guttercat would be there, burns and all. He smiled weakly, gave me a cat-bat salute, and said, "Thank you, Casey, it's great to be around you and the crew. Guess I needed something to wake me up."

I said, "We're all glad to have you. Even more so since you now know your ass from a hole in the ground. Go and get some pretty pussycat to clean up those wounds, and we'll see you tonight." More stand-up swift cat-bat saluting ensued, with nary a smile. Shortly after leaving, much hearty cat laughing occurred quite far away from where I was. 'Nuff to make a cat smile.

The chimney meeting was held in its usual beautiful surroundings. The sights and sounds of the city engulfed us. The fog and sea smell threw on another blanket. The meeting was short, and we all decided at once what must be done. Truth is stranger than fiction. We had to speak to the most important man in the world. Once it was Eisenhower, and now it was...Sean Connery. He lives on the East Coast, on the very coast, one hundred yards from the sea at high tide. He can have, if all else fails, immediate exit by helicopter, ship, or submarine. The house is actually a triple-fortified bomb shelter with a basement and a tunnel eighty feet under the house that leads out into the ocean floor, where there is another shelter that Sean hopes he never has to visit. It controls all the lethal weapons in the world. Further thought as to what might happen would be useless. If he has to go there, he will know what to do. Contacting him is almost impossible, but not for us. Sean has two cats. We have about one thousand "helpers" in the area. (This is the most important place in the world, after all, and we don't want to be a cat hair surprised.) The order was given to get Jiggs the cat. Jiggs and Mercy are the two cats Sean is crazy about. Jiggs would be given certain telepathic powers that would let Sean know what was happening, and even more so, to take immediate action, like yesterday. Yeah.

Jiggs did the job right away. He brushed over Sean's hand on the side table where he was about to have one more tiny nip of the good stuff and call it a day. His hand no more than touched the glass when he remembered a memo from "on top." It said that area was sensitive and not well guarded. Think tank had it right up there with all the great cities in the world. Sean pushed a button, and five other men answered the phone immediately. It was through a chip in their heads that they could be called by Sean anytime there was a "situation." This situation was discussed and the problem stated, as was a solution. In five minutes the entire accelerator and a five-mile radius around it were completely covered. Persuasive war tactics would be used on anybody who seemed to be doing something unusual. This was WAR! Everything was covered in the air, on the ground, and on the beach next to the accelerator. In five more minutes, everything was under control. All the enemies were captured or killed. They would be dealt with when all information was given and recorded. The chief interrogators don't use waterboarding anymore. They use what works immediately. It is a highly secret truth serum, a blended chemical that is sprayed in the mouth. The enemies talk right away, and they tell everything with no holding back. They cannot help themselves.

The next morning, everything was completely under control only by those who controlled it, and our enemies, of course. But now we knew who they were, and they knew nothing of us. It's us cats! Yeaaaaaaaaaaaa, we are the final ones that really rule the world. Jiggs and Mercy were sitting by the fireplace as Sean was watching his favorite movie by Orson Welles, *The Third Man*. He loved the song and looking at the wet streets of Paris he had been on and loved many times before. He had to get up to go to the kitchen for one more. Whatta day, and yet terribly mysterious, definitely a four-helper day. Upon coming back to watch the movie, he saw Jiggs and Mercy sitting on either arm of his large leather chair. He smiled the James Bond smile as he sat down, petted both simultaneously, and gave them some Welsh wisdom. He started out with a low chuckle, and ended laughing, long, loud, and deep. Very deep! (Dare I say even, yes, tiger like?) With great camaraderie and caring, he put each cat on the seat of his favorite leather chair by the fireplace where he sat often to look at the sea and watch his movies. He pulled up a dining chair, sat down, and while continuing to laugh, he looked knowingly and humorously into each cat's eyes and said, "The jig is up!" He then finished by saying, "Anybody want to have a drink before the next movie?" 'Nuff to make a cat laugh! Now, how about that easy meal and a ride to the moon?

Night at the Movies

*L*ast night was wonderful! John was fast asleep and I was sitting on his back watching *Bell, Book, & Candle*! The cast in the show was tremendous! I had to turn up the volume as John was "purring" a bit too loudly. Once when the cat looked into the camera, I caught a quick glimpse of her mind. Fascinating! She had some idea of what she was doing, and was enjoying herself immensely. She reminded me of me, and I'm glad John was sleeping and did not see that cat, or he would have taken me right to Warner Bros and tried to put me into a movie. I could, but for some reason, it doesn't appeal to me. I think John would get disturbed and question my loyalty if I won an animal Oscar or whatever. Like I said, I have to keep a close eye on him. Where else can you get a deal like this? Don't forget the fridge and car rides. Forget all the butter. "Awctually" I like them, but I must meow a bit to keep my cover, thin as it is getting.

Cat Instincts

$\mathcal{A}$lthough I can read minds, I am still a cat and have insatiable curiosity about everything. As John was taking a shower, my place of denial, I saw the shower curtains moving back and forth. Fascinating to me! Instantly all my cat instincts came alive, and I bounded from the commode to the sink, to the top of the shower curtain. YEAAA! Now I was doing what I was born to do! Investigate. All my claws dug into the plastic curtain, and instantly, I was in the shower with John! I bought myself another bath. Being a cat has its drawbacks; and sometimes I wish I was human to at least be able to drive a car.

John has been trying to move from the desert to the beach. I must make sure we go when I want. I am using my subliminal suggestion on him often. When he thinks of a place I like, I meow, look at him, and move my mink tail slowly back and forth. He looks at me and smiles and pets me. Soon, I will have him completely under my control. Then what?! I already have all I could ever need. Then again, if somehow I could get my own office. Being a world-renowned cat psychologist might be fun with all that money and fame. On second thought, I better not. John would laugh himself to death when he would see me smoking a pipe, wearing glasses, and meowing in a German accent, too much grist for the mill. Sometimes being a mind-reading cat is overwhelming. I'll just get John to take me for a ride and put my paws on the steering wheel and look hypnotically into the oncoming traffic. Either that or go into the fridge and have lunch. Hmmm, think I'll have lunch first and then cat-drive the car.

The shows on TV can make a cat laugh! Nonsense at best! I cat pawed—cats don't stumble—upon some religious shows, and some were interesting for about three seconds. One preacher kind of looked like a cat in the way he moved his hands this way and that, like I move my tail. He also tried to use the cat staring hypnotic look, but it didn't work on me. Then I had it figured out! This human was trying to evolve into a cat! Only problem was that his first go-around would be like nutty Uncle Al. He already reminded me so much of Al that I realized I had made another major cat breakthrough in evolution. Cats rule! Believe me, this preacher was about to turn into a cat before my very paws and mink coat! He thought he was speaking English, but he wasn't. He had some kind of a heavy Okie accent, mispronouncing every word, and would yell, "Amen!" Just like nutty Uncle Al when he is wasted on catnip and looking for bird eggs to suck. I turned the channel to another preacher, and he was doing the same thing. One channel after another had nutty Al imitators saying, "Amen! Amen!" all the time. Substitute "Amen" for "Meow," with their attempted hypnotic gaze and vacuous babble, not to mention balding heads, and you have you know who. On thoughtful cat insight, these ways of humans will not, I say, will cat-never evolve into cats. Maybe into bedbugs, but never into cats. All cats want is a free ride, a mink coat, and a nice tail with eighteen sharp claws. The humans bit off way too much and are at great risk of turning into kitty litter. Figure they speak in reverse. They see things in reverse. They got the ends of a cat confused as to what part they wanted to be. I quickly switched over to *Twilight Zone* and the Sid Caesar show. Ahhh, cat reality is so refreshing!

Air Cat Carrier

I was doing what cats do when I received a meow from Uncle Al. He wanted to talk about being a jet pilot—more precisely, an aircraft jet pilot. His questions were what one would expect from Al. "Where's a carrier and where's a jet that jumps off it?" I said, "No problem." We went down to San Diego to see what cats will see. Uncle Al loved it! There were planes and so much noise and the smell of oil.

Uncle Al and I waited until dark, and then he said, "Come aboard." It was quiet and orderly, and we found the planes in no time. We jumped into the cockpits and immediately had it cat-fig-ured out as to how to fly the jet. "Wow!" Al said. "Let's go!" We pulled all the necessary levers, put on our specially made oxygen masks, and roared right off the deck. We looked back, and there was much confusion, but so what? You leave the door to an F-14 aircraft open on a carrier, and someone is bound to give it a try.

Uncle Al Wants to Travel

I like to travel, and what cat doesn't? John has to help me get through customs and provide transportation to and fro, but that is that. He does the work, and I run the show. I think John knows it, and I think he likes it. I hear him laughing at night, so I know I am doing the right thing.

But, there is Uncle Al. He let me know he has a cruise ship ready to go, and we can get on and go to Europe. Voila, plenty of food, comfort, sights, and places to clean up. What else is there? I'm not all that sure of this trip, so Al is doing his best to tell me that it is just what I need. Hmmmmm? One thing for sure about Al, and that is that he is always, *capital Always*, doing misdirection plays, his specialty. So, what's the hang-up? The hang-up is that I don't know what Al is really thinking, and I don't want to be involved in hijacking an ocean liner. (Would you believe me being caught, and then sentenced to be put in an animal shelter for too long?) Al says all is cool—his adjective, not mine...like ever—and that we will never have a better time, and that the ship leaves tomorrow. So, I think it over and say, "Okay, now to pack!" We will be leaving tomorrow morning, and I want to make sure John is settled down and everything is in place.

I came in the bedroom to see how John was doing, and he said, "Hello, cathead," and tugged on my tail. He was watching a Bogart movie, and it was a good one, *Casablanca*. John was making comments to the actors as the show began, and I laughed a bit. He was using his phony German accent and saying things to Ingrid Bergman that were borderline sexy. No, they were completely sexy on second thought. He sang along to the song "As Time Goes By" and tried to get a meow out of me, so what the heck, I gave him one, medium length and medium sound. He said, "Very good," and that I must be in a good mood, and why don't I dress up and go to Hollywood, and blah blah blah. I laughed some more and rolled over so he couldn't tell I was laughing, and batted the air with my cat paws, which I know he likes. I thought before I left I would make him happy, so when I came back he would remember and feed me. He was munching on some kind of crackers with liquid garlic on them, and he offered me one. I thought since I would be going I might as well take a bite and that would make him feel he knows what I like to eat. Wow, was that cracker a bomb! It went all the way down, and I jumped on the couch and batted the air some more and waved my tail around vigorously. He laughed, got me some water, and I took a sip. No more crackers, thank you! He knew it was more than I needed too, he told me, and gave me a pet. The show continued, and we sat on the couch and enjoyed the movie. How good can it get?

I was due to leave in five hours, so I lay down to get some sleep so I would not be a grouchy passenger. (Humans have to pay about ten thousand dollars for the grand trip. Cats go for free!) John put a small blanket over me and growled like a mountain lion as he left the room and laughed, and so did I. (He is always telling jokes.) About three hours later, there was a noise coming from the bedroom, and I went to check. John was making funny noises and moving about in an agitated fashion. I took a brief mental glimpse, and he was very worried about me. Why? I was feeling great, but he sensed something. It had to be a mistake, and I walked over, and on top of him, and checked him out. All checked out okay. Hmmm, I couldn't go off around the world with John not feeling good and depending on me for all kinds of support. Uncle Al showed up at that time, and we discussed the situation. "What the phooey," he said. "The ships leave every day. Let's get the old boy back on his feet," Al said, "and find out what is going on. Maybe we can take him with us."

Hey, good idea. Then again, I began to worry about all the beautiful European women who would go crazy for John. Why they like a guy like that I have no idea. He sings, laughs, drives a car, tells me jokes, goes to restaurants, reads books, goes swimming every day, and tells people all kinds of Irish malarkey wherever he is. Oh, I know, it is me. Women love me in the backpack and always ask this and that about me, and I never know what he is going to tell them. I like the story where he says I am a baby mountain lion, and he has one month to go before he has to turn me into the wild. I had to duck into the backpack and laugh for about a minute when I heard that one, and when I stuck my head out, my eyes were all teary and weeping. The woman said, "Yes, the cat showed signs of being a vicious beast, and can I pet him please before you have to leave?"

"Careful," John said, and I had to duck down again and laugh. She reached in, took me out, and petted me. Such beautiful-smelling perfume was wafting around her. I had to live up to my BS reputation, so I cat-batted her shoulder and John said not to worry, that I was only stretching, and I had never encountered a human female. I was overloaded. I crawled up on her shoulder and looked at John, and he was laughing. I just had to stay there and get petted and smell 400-dollar perfume for about a minute. I took a brief glance into her head, and his as well, and cancelled the trip with Al. This was going to be so much better. When I found her perfume, I would transfer some to Al for backing out on the trip. Believe me, sometimes ole Al needs all the perfume he can get. 'Nuff to make a cat laugh!

The Launching of the Casey

*J*ohn had named the boat after me, not knowing that I could read and understand every word that was spoken not only by him, as well as any language in the world, maybe even alien. I heard they communicate mentally, so I guess I can speak to them as well. It was going to be a perfect day. The weather gods, wind, water, temperature, and tide all coincided to make it one of the most memorable sailing days in a long time. Cats are quite reserved or maybe completely bored, but the night before the launching, the Coco Cabanas were in abundance. Many of my friends and their friends dropped by, and I let out a couple of big "Meows" and waved my tail with enthusiasm. The big seagulls were emitting their low-voiced caw caws, with a few blasts in between. The cats were smoking their cigars, waving their tails, and of course, Uncle Al was doing a little cha cha cha.

All of a sudden a deck of cards appeared, and we all took seats and began playing cards. Small bets, large bets, no bets, crazy bets—just any kind of a bet would do. Seagull Joe claimed to have won a hand, and he flapped his very big wings and put out some of the Coco Cabanas. One of the young cats thought he won a pot and did a backflip right into the water. We were going great, and it was impossible to imagine how much better life could be. Sailors must go to sleep, we had read somewhere, so the party "tailed" off, and only the slap, slap of the water against the hull and the occasional meow of a young cat or the loud caw of a seagull could be heard. Seagull Joe said he would fly above and make sure all was okay. Uncle Al was stuffing his pockets with lots of sardines that he had won from the young cats.

The beautiful *Casey* was ready to go. It was a full moon and the last vestiges of blue-gray were whisked away by the sea breeze, leaving only the smells of the ocean. Finally, I was going to sea on my "own" boat to see other lands, seek adventure, do what must be done, and what the heck, I was a tired cat. I went into the cabin and fell asleep on the captain's chair. A few small meows, some purring, and I was off to dream land. My dreams were unlike any I had ever had. I had never slept on the sea before, so different things were to be expected.

I took a walk around the boat and made sure all was secure, especially John. How could I sail this thing without him? Uncle Al, Seagull Joe, and I had never sailed a boat, so John was very important. No rum rum or diddly dum dum for him. I went to where he was sleeping and brushed my whiskers against his face to see how he was feeling. He was dreaming about still trying to make a basketball shot he had missed about thirty years ago. John was the perfect captain, no pressure whatsoever. All was set at five bells, and we anchored away. Many of my friends were on the catwalk. See, I was born to sail, and we pulled out with nary a hitch. We were going to clear the harbor, go north just by the Faralon Islands, and then head straight to Hawaii. John was thinking about doing the Tom Selleck/ Magnum thing, and I was as happy as when I was born with all my eleven brothers and sisters. Constant warmth, food, and our mother telling us to be careful about absolutely everything. So much meowing and purring, tail wagging, and the occasional cat-bat by Mom when one of us cats got out of line, simply wonderful.

About thirty minutes later all was well, and the western breeze was slowly blowing against us as the sun was rising in the southeast. I jumped up next to the wheel so I could get a clear look at where we were going. I heard John singing something by Sinatra, and then he pointed out to sea and said, "There she blows!" It was a great blue whale, and it came and circled our boat so close that I could see it smile. We had a conversation about her children. She had two, and she was fifteen years old. They were going to Hawaii, too. She said she and her friends would keep watch on us for the entire trip, and if there was anything we needed, to let her know. She had been at sea her entire life and had never had such an exhilarating conversation as ours. She told me about absolutely everything. We all know how mothers are. She just kept talking and talking, and oh boy! It was great, but how do you tell a twenty-ton whale you have had enough mom talk? She kept asking me question after question, and I told her about our miracle cigars and that she was welcome to have one. She giggled and said sure, but don't tell the kids. I got out a super big cigar and placed it in her mouth. Then, she ate it! I then had to light one up for myself and show her how to smoke it properly. She said, "Hold on a minute, I think I have an idea." She came up shortly with a five-foot piece of pipe, and we stuck the cigar in the end and lit it. Voila! Soon, she was puffing, smiling, breeching, talking, and laughing all at once. After about twenty cigars, she seemed satisfied and told me that wherever she went, she would tell the rest of her friends what a tremendous cigar this was, and could she "represent us"? What do you say to a twenty-ton whale that is twice as big as your boat, totally loaded, making whale sounds, and also wants to be your best salesman. Oops, better say sales lady here. A deal was done. "Come and visit at your convenience," I said and knocked a few clams off her hide before she went away. A true dear she was, but I really needed Uncle Al negotiating for that one.

We were nearing the Faralon Islands, and I began to feel like I had too much of what I drank out of John's glass that one night that I thought was water, only worse. I was pale afterward. My fur was getting stiff. I meowed big time, fell over, and John picked me up. He told me I was sick and that we had to go back. We went back as quickly as possible, but the trip was made worse when I saw a school of sardines. (Couldn't be a school, because nothing that went to school would stink that bad.) I wanted to die, and then some. Nothing could make me happy. Not cigars, meowing at the moon, cheating at cards, reading John's mind when he was sleeping, my favorite Steve McQueen show, ice cream, watching Al do the cha-cha at the Kasbah, or looking at my greatness in a mirror. Simply nothing. I wanted my mom. I wanted to die. I believed in God. I would never steal treats from the store again. I promised the moon and the stars and…and then John began to sing Sinatra, beautiful Sinatra music. In my condition he sounded like Caruso and Sinatra wrapped into one. He sang the great and lyrical song "This Love of Mine," and I was so happy. I listened in a *cat*-a-tonic state until we reached shore. That will be my favorite song forever. So enchanting, so wonderful, and boy, did it help my tummy calm down.

Word had reached shore that we were on our way with one very sick cat, and the vet was there with all a cat needed. He gave me a shot and smelled my breath and said to John, "Why does this cat's breath smell like tobacco? Don't you know it is illegal to let cats smoke on boats?"

John said, "I am well aware of that sailing statute, and to the best of my knowledge, he has never smoked a cigarette in his life."

More of that kind of talk and I would become sick again, so I "suggested" to the doctor in place of his vet bill to have three cigars and call it even. The doc agreed and lit up. In no time at all, he was moving in a languid manner that resembled the cha-cha and humming "They play the tuba down in Cuba." Close call again. Ahem! Soon, all was normal. We made sure we would get the proper "stuff" the next time we went sailing, but you know how cats are. (I'm almost wishing I did.)

Uncle Al, Seagull Joe, and I met at the chimney, which is the most perfect spot in the entire world to see and think on a full moon night. I told them what happened. Uncle Al said he already knew what happened, and I said, "How could you?" He went on to say that everybody has heard of snow cats, but that he was a "stow" cat. Seagull Joe almost choked on his Coco Cabana, and some little cats that had snuck up with Uncle Al started laughing and meowing so uproariously that I left. Stow cats, indeed! Humph!

Casey Sez

I had a very busy day today, what with it being the first of the month and all. I had to make sure I had my pedicure appointment, was on schedule, and that John changed the oil in the car every 3,000 miles, plus a nail cutting and teeth cleaning for me. I demand it. So does John. Sometimes John goes to the barber, and I get a kick out of that. We go into the shop, and he puts me on a chair, and I pretend to sleep. All the people get real quiet, but because I am wearing my cat care tail coverall, everything is okay.

Once someone asked John about what I do, and so forth. John says things like this: "He's very calming. He has heart pills taped to his tail in case I have a heart attack, and then there is his ability to make a huge sound like a Burmese tiger if we get in any kind of trouble." (John couldn't or wouldn't stop me from guarding him.) He said I cost a lot of money, and that his psychiatrist (who is really me, but he doesn't know it) said John was a cat man (it took some doing on my part to get that done), and that I would be perfect for him. I was only four months old at the time when he showed up at the pound and chose me from about thirty other cats. (you see, John isn't the only storyteller around here…smiles) I already had my mind-reading abilities, so it was no trouble getting him to choose me. It was more the other way around. I had been there for about a month, and I had only recently known of my mind-reading abilities. I thought all cats had it but soon learned otherwise, and it took me some time, about ten minutes, to know how to use it properly. So many people wanted me because they say I am so pretty. First of all, I am a male cat, and I don't like being thought of as "pretty." Handsome maybe… Then they wanted me because of my big, beautiful blue eyes, and tail, and teeth, because humans tend to have bugs and stuff in their homes, and they think that is just what is needed for (catching bugs) doing that chore. Yucko! There were all kinds of reasons they wanted me, but the last one I will tell you is that they wanted me for their children. Simply, I don't like the odor of you know what, wearing doll clothes, being carried around like a baby, and I don't like yelling and crying, night and day, and that's enough. How on earth would I sneak in my catnaps at that rate? No, that was not going to be the life for me.

I was ready to leave, as I was getting stronger and faster by the day, but since I also have the talent to see into the future, I knew John would show up very soon. As yet, my ability to see the future wasn't perfected, and I had to wait, sleep, and wait, and try not to let the scatterbrained thoughts of people passing by lead me to distraction. Most remarkable since I was only a four-month-old kitten. Meow-Ha-Ha! Then "It happened," as the song goes. If there isn't a song by that name, I will tell John, and he will walk in and start looking at all of us as if we will write it down while sleeping or crawling or doing other cat stuff.

John immediately went over to a big alley cat who head-butted him as a sign of affection. John laughed and thought a minute. Remember, I could read minds very well even at four months. Whattacat! He kept walking my direction and went right to where I was sitting at eye level on a catwalk. (Yes, I had something to do with it!) We looked at each other, and he was what I wanted. What he didn't have, I could teach him. I knew he was very trainable. He picked me up gently, petted my stomach, and asked the attendant if

I was available, and if I had any "problems." They said I was fine, had all my shots, and was good to go, so off we went for my first car ride home. I "heard" John thinking, and it was funny. 'Nuff to make a cat laugh!

Two in One

Sometimes my ability to read minds is not the cat's meow. Believe me, just you believe me (as my dear mother used to say to her legion of kitties), it has its drawbacks. Most people are thinking absolutely nothing. Animals are thinking about food. Hummmmm. Humans think about food quite a bit also, so... No, I won't go there, not yet. I know you probably think, "Oh, I would love to read minds." For a comparison, I will use a Catholic priest hearing confession. Oh goody, everyone says, that must be so much fun. But think it through, dear reader. Hearing confession is listening to all the junk and flotsam and jetsam of humanity, not fun. After a while, it becomes so predictable, sometimes disturbing, and even boring. Guess a shrink has the same kind of shtick. Pays much, much better, and he says, "Give me lots of money" instead of five Hail Marys. Oy vey, such a deal!

John took me shopping to a giant store, and I just went to sleep. Don't worry now, my cat sensors are always on. You don't get to be the smartest cat in the universe by sleeping on the job. My sleep was moving along quite well. John was getting this and that, and cussing at most everything. Funneeeee! Like why do they put it here, and why do they put it there, and why does the wheel on this cart make noise? He was looking for a Bose radio in a pharmacy. I had to laugh so hard that I was moving around considerably. John liked it. He thought I was scratching his back, which made me laugh more. I had to come up for air. Phew! It was really a boring store. It was about seven at night, and you could tell the shoppers were finishing their day. They were tired, and the workers simply wanted to run away and hide. It's called hating one's job, a frequent attitude with so many people who have to work and find themselves stuck in a funky job, like a priest or a shrink. Oops, guess I better watch what I say. (I would love to comment more on our first amendment rights, but you don't have time to read an entire encyclopedia under "R" for rights, and I don't want to wake up any morons. George Orwell, you said it all.)

We were working our way through the line at the checkout stand, and there was a lady in front of us getting stuff and tapping her jeweled rings loudly on the cart's push bar. The man in front of her was about six and a half feet tall, wearing a tan rain coat and a derby. He looked a lot like the inspector in the Sherlock Holmes movies (I love those movies!) or even the arch villain, Moriarity. Boy, was he ever an evil cat! World domination, bad music, and nobody was too small to hate or kill. He killed his gardener for not watering a specific plant, and no, it wasn't *that* type of plant. The man had a peculiar way about him. His movements seemed to be out of synch. Everybody can't move like I can, so I hardly paid attention, but my cat sensors were beginning to almost glow. I took a quick peep under his derby and got two minds going at once. Huh? It was two midgets, one standing upon another and moving about like a six-foot-six person. The two midgets were thinking about nothing but evil. Especially the midget who was on the bottom, but that was for an entirely different reason. It seems the midget on top—they took turns—was lax in his toiletry duties and, well…'nuff said.

I communicated to John that something very strange and evil was afoot (literally…pardon the pun…and more of the upcoming ones as well). I just can't get over John shopping for a Boze radio in Walgreens. But, hey, that's why I like him so much, I think. Ha!

Ha! He "heard' me and kept a surreptitious eye on the man with the derby. The woman in front of us had by now dropped her purse on the floor while looking for her cell phone, and looked at John as if to say, "Pick it up, you oaf!" He was all ready to do it, but we had to get going. The man (the midgets, the derby) was heading out the door, after shortchanging the clerk, mind you. He gave her a ten and after getting change, he said it was a twenty. I knew then we had our paws full. We left our cart, and the woman with metal and stones and paint all over her hands, as well. All we had in the cart was yogurt and a toilet brush. (Boy, is John a shopper or what?)

We went out the door after "the Derby" and watched where he went. Not hard to follow his car. It was a Rolls. The Derby got in the backseat, and off they went. With our specially designed laser pencil, we were able to put a mark on the car, "Excuuuuuuse me, the Rolls," and follow it no matter where it went on the entire planet, outer space for that matter. From what I just saw, I would not be surprised. They drove four blocks to a fifteen-story condo building and went into the garage. We watched them go in and then decided to check out this Derby character. His, their, well…the Derby was named Rufus Weatherbee. (should have known.) "He" had lived there for three years, traveled all the time, and had nine other places around the planet. Had his own plane and a crew of workers to keep his business and residences up and running 24/7. He was an international attorney who had clients all over the world, spoke many different languages, and had friends in various governments. Boring, but not everybody can be a cat. There was no doubt about it, Rufus, the Derby, the midgets, and the attorney were up to some wild stuff, and we were going to find out what it was. (Teach him to shortchange checkout clerks.)

This was a very unusual, but terribly interesting situation. I decided to call in my friends for a meeting by the chimney at midnight.

All of the crew would be there—Seagull Joe, Uncle Al, and his group of "startups" (sometimes I want to call them something other than "startups") and Havana cigars for all. We would enjoy the great San Francisco view, the faint far-off sounds of Tony Bennett singing you know what song, and maybe "Cat" King Cole getting crazy under an orange-colored sky. It all was going swimmingly, as Seagull Joe liked to say, as Al began to laugh at some of the protégés he brought with him. One of them was laughing so hard at what he heard about the midgets and the Derby that he fell into the chimney. We pulled him out, dusted him off, and threatened him. He laughed even more. Obviously, that protégé was going to be a great success. Seagull Joe went "Caw caw" a few times (his way of saying, "I think I have it") and said he and his minions could monitor the Derby no matter where he went. Seagulls cover the planet. (In more ways than one… Ahem.) Uncle Al and his helpers would be the paws on the ground wherever the Derby went, and of course, I would be the coordinator. One of the protégés shouted out, "He is the brains of the outfit!" and more laughter and cigar smoke ensued. (By golly, I am really beginning to like Al's "men.")

By following the Derby night and day, we would find out what he was up to, and methinks it is not a good up to. Why would anyone take turns standing on another's shoulders, one not properly sanitized, cheat checkout clerks, lie about one's name, and do who knows what all, while traveling around the planet? All you have to do is stay at home, hack into Chase Manhattan, and cheat the world—too easy probably. Guess you just have to like your work.

Reports were coming in with all kinds of meows and caw caws. One of the protégés was thrown into a garbage truck while trying to use it as a springboard to get on the Derby's balcony. Perfect cover since cats falling into garbage trucks is common. Quite the brilliant move by that protégé. (Excuse me, but I had to laugh at one of my own for quite a while. First, the chimney and now the garbage truck. Maybe we should put him in records. Probably set the place on fire in no time. Got to love it!)

The Derby continued to move all over the planet, one country after another. One midget on top of the other and then they changed places. We called them Big Stinky and Little Stinky. Whatta way to do whatever they were doing! But what were they doing? As it so often happens, it took a rookie, yes, a protégé, to find out what the Derby was doin'. Oh, yeah! He had fallen asleep, what a surprise, at the bottom of the garbage chute that goes up and down the entire building. While examining the garbage, as he put it, one of the midgets came shooting down the chute, hit the garbage pile, and took off on a motorcycle. Vrooooom! Vrooooom! No problem. Seagull Joe and company followed him wherever he went. Meanwhile, the other midget shot down the chute and did the same motorcycle exit. He was followed as well. They were going all over the city, in and out of every building, with phony IDs, sometimes exiting with cycles and other times with cars or limousines. Often they would coordinate and become the Derby. This went on all over the world. What were they doing? Really?

We found out. They were earning a living the hard way. They earned it. With their disguise as the Derby, they were entirely free to go about wherever they wanted as midgets. In some cultures they were as big as the inhabitants and not considered midgets. In other cultures they became the Derby. They sold warheads to countries around the world as the Derby, or as themselves, with various make-overs to blend in. For example, in China they would pull a rickshaw, and in London they would be doormen. If nothing else, they always had the garbage chutes and the Derby. I was astounded at their cleverness. Actually, besides the fact we saw them cheating a checkout clerk, all they did was go around the world and sell warheads to whomever wanted them. They were given huge amounts of money, and the cycle continued. Warheads, money, and money and warheads. The countries receiving the warheads did not have delivery capability for the warheads, but they would tell their people they had them. They felt secure. What's a few billion or zillion dollars to keep control of your country? It's the people's money. Not the dictators'. Everybody was happy.

I took all our reports and told John about it. I said, "Let's go to whomever is in charge of the show here and tell them what we know." (A few shekels on the side would be appreciated...ahem.) We checked around with Seagull Joe and paws on the ground. In one day we found out who is actually the leader of this country, of the world actually. He lives in Kennebunkport, right on the beach. (Good place for a helicopter to land, and a ship or sub to be quite handy). It is Sean Connery. A seagull spotted certain activity that could only be done by the leader of the world, and paws on the ground spoke to his cat, and he meowed all over the place. Happy to do it! He and his family, and their family, get caviar forever, the best Russian kind.

It was too much. John went directly to the house. Wearing elevator shoes, a tan coat, derby hat, and driving a Rolls-Royce. He was let in immediately and politely showed into the living room looking out over the ocean, served tea and some kind of a cigar. Sean walked in and said, "Well, now, what have we been up to that brings you here?" He was smiling. John smiled as well and told him who he and I were because I was in the coat as well. I "communicated' with Sean Connery and made several "suggestions." The jig was up, as Bogart used to say, and what do you have to say for yourself? Sean said, "Simple (in his Welsh accent it came out "schimple"...loved it). The United States sells defunct warheads all around the world for zillions of dollars and commitments from dictatorships. They are able to keep their minions in line and keep their heads. We pay off the national debt and have zillions more in reserve for what may come. Anything else?"

John said, "This is a terrible cigar! Let me show you what I have!"

"Meow!"

Super Bowl 49

I wish cats could play football. Well, actually, we can, but from what I am seeing and hearing, it sounds like a mess, except for the trillion paws that will be made by betting in Las Vegas. That will get Uncle Al's attention. Wherever there is any kind of action anywhere, Al is there. This year Super Bowl 49, they are very worried about enough air being in the footballs?! Perfect! Cat heaven! Put us in charge of footballs. We will take bribes from everybody. Each of us will carry three footballs on our back with a sack on our side; put the money in the cat sack, tell us how much air you want, and it is done. Of course, we will keep the money, and what do we know about air and footballs? When the quarterback bends over, he will have three cats to choose from, each one carrying three footballs, and he can put the dough in the sack after he has chosen what he wants. Again, perfect! There will be cats all over, looking exactly alike, ready to sell, er, provide anybody with a ball. We will be sure the kickers, the catchers, the center, the coaches, and the officials will all have a chance at any time to get a football. Retainer will be required, of course. We will run all over the field, before, during, and after the game, with cat speed, cordiality, and a proper meow and eye contact made upon each transaction. It will be the smoothest run football hand line ever seen or conceived.

I have also read, heard, and seen that much trickery has been going on with football, on all levels, on and off the field, for almost a hundred years. I understand that I will be in charge, with Uncle Al carrying out special assignments. As catnip is our kryptonite, so are women to most, anyhow, ahem, football players. The night before a game, a cat mind-meld will occur with everyone who is associated with the game. Once the game begins, it will be played with great beauty, speed, and enthusiasm of such magnitude that any issue of misconduct would not even move a cat's whisker.

All will be beautiful and written about in the sports columns as being truly and undoubtedly the greatest game ever. Yes, I had to "visit" the writers as well, and in some instances, I could not resist some "advice." After all, I fancy my writing with quite a lot of Twain, and he would be proud of me. After the game and festivities had been completed, and delicately orchestrated by me, ahem, there was a soft wind engulfing all those to whom this game meant even an iota. They all talked about the game, laughed, and became animated and more pleased with themselves and others than they had ever been before. I almost worried for an instant if I had put too much human catnip in the breeze. Not a mention was made or even remembered of the great number of kitty cats that controlled every aspect in and around the game worldwide. Only one, no, *two* close calls occurred.

Uncle Al was on special assignment of the restrooms. In this case, they were used for betting and buying footballs by my legion of meowing helpers. It seems if Al did not get $1,000 for a football, he would have his "special guard" of seagulls give the chiseler, man or woman, a ride into the Pacific. I just told him to put some catnip, the human version, on their shoes, one meow, and he would get twice as much. Worked like a charm, as only Al can be. Doubled up the catnip and for $5,000, he would also give them the water ride. After all, the seagulls were bored, and they enjoyed the exercise. Five to a person and they got some free sardines. I transgress, guess that was more than a close call. But Uncle Al is my top cat, and he depends on using the seagulls to go to Europe frequently. Looks like I am a little bit like a Super Bowl executive after all. Al did it. It wasn't me, and you can't prove a thing anyhow. Meow!

Crazy Uncle Al Strikes Again

*C*razy Uncle Al is always doing something that humans would deem to be illegal. Being a cat, he is only doing what cats do naturally. Well, it is what Al does anyhow. Yesterday, he brought over a chicken and gave me his big "Meow!" He was on top of the roof with a chicken he had caught, and he said, "Let's eat!" I said, "No, thank you," and asked him where he got it. He said it was from a chicken truck that he visits frequently. He said he just jumps on the truck when it goes by and helps himself and jumps off. He said they only chased him once, and he has been doing it for years. Meanwhile, Al had feathers all over his face and was rapidly gnawing away, having a good time. At that time, John was going into the house and saw the feathers coming down from the roof. I ducked away just in time and came back into the house via my secret entrance. When John sat down, I meowed and got on his lap, walked up his arm and over his shoulder, then again, back to his lap, so I could do mind-reading on what John was thinking and use my cat distraction technique to get any Al thoughts out of his mind. Ahem! Feathers and all!

The Pyramids

*H*ave you been to the pyramids? The ones in Egypt I mean. There are pyramids all over the world and lots in the eastern United States, but none as famous as the ones in Egypt. It seems the ones in Egypt are very hard to explore because there are all sorts and sizes of tunnels going through them in every which way. Some of these tunnels are only big enough for a small animal or a cat to fit through. I wish John had never found that out. Until his eternal search to put me in Hollywood as some kind of a dumb cat that yells and has a bell around its neck comes along, he is thinking about jamming me in a tunnel in one of the biggest rock piles on the planet. Okay already, so he got a boat for me that almost killed me, and now he thinks because he gave me a boat, which is really our boat, that he can use me in some way to make money. I know Uncle Al would be good for the job, but after he saw the first dead King Tut, he would jump on Joe Seagull Air Taxi and leave that weird place.

John was sure this plan would work. We would contact some people he had read about in National Geographic, and they would be overjoyed at his idea to put his wonderfully trained cat in one of those mile-long dark tunnels. Why, who knows, what with the Egyptians reverence for cats, I might become some kind of a cat pharaoh and get my picture on the cover of *The Rolling Stone*? So, it's off to the pile of rocks, and let the devil take the hindmost. (I have heard and read that phrase before, and I finally got a chance to use it. Perfect place for a devil anyhow.) We got our stuff together, which mainly consisted of my orange cat care jacket and a passport, and off we flew. John demanded that I ride with him up front because of his "condition." (I would now call it animal cruelty, although he thought of it as my being his service cat.) I had pills in the pockets of my jacket that were necessary immediately if his "condition" kicked in. The story went that I had to be with him every second, as such was the nature of his situation. Since nowadays everyone is scream- ing animal care this and animal care that, it was easy enough to do. As the saying goes, if only cats could talk. The first thing I would say is that I don't want to go in those dirty, scary, suffocating, claus- trophobic tunnels. But, here I am flying first class, posing as some kind of a human helper when I thought all this animal talk stuff was about taking care of animals.

We landed and went immediately to the pyramids. Our trip had been meticulously laid out for us, so everything was ready to go the moment our truck pulled up to the biggest pyramid in the world. We were escorted to the opening to the tunnel, and in I went. I figured it would only take as long as I wanted it to, so what the heck? Who did they think they were dealing with? That crazy boat got me into this situation to begin with, and I was beginning to get my "cat up." The tunnel was surprisingly cool, and with my great vision plus the small light I had on my back, I was able to move along at a slow trot. Up ahead I heard some sounds and immediately stopped. The light was activated by movement, so it went off. I was then able to use my mind-reading ability to see what was going on. It turned out to be a couple of rats who lived there, and they were having a casual con- versation. Perfect! I made a small noise so as to not frighten them and communicated by mental telepathy what I was "told" to do and did they have any ideas? Boy, did they ever! They were first of all sorry that I was being mistreated, and since it was necessary for me to prove I was doing something in the middle of where nobody had ever been, they knew just what to do. As it turned out, they were on the governing board of the animal activist party and were fighting with every tooth and tail to make sure their rights were heard and given the attention they deserved.

Their names were Tut I and Tut II, really. I forged right ahead and asked, "What plan do you have to further our animal rights and prove to my 'master' that I am actually getting something done?"

Tut II said, "There is nothing here but miles and miles of tunnels that were built for ventilation. They lead to various rooms which we will show you, and maybe we can work something out."

Sounded more and more like something Al would do, but here I was. The rooms they showed me were the worse for wear, with skeletons all over and, I might add, tons and tons of gold, diamonds, precious stones. And behold, two skeletons of my brethren. Tut I and Tut II noticed my reaction and sadness and said, "We are all brethren down here. In fact every animal is our brethren. The sooner we start treating each other with kindness and understanding, instead of eating each other, the sooner will our rights be accepted and acted upon." The air was thick in this room, as was the conversation, so I said, "You are absolutely right, and now what can we do?" Tut I said, "Humans are crazy about all of the riches that are piled up in the room, and maybe we can make a deal." Deal, my favorite word…

They put a couple million dollars' worth of diamonds in my jacket, which amounted to four ounces, and back I went. Upon exiting the tunnel, I was engulfed by flashbulb lights and oohs and ahhs, and a cup of stale camel milk. I was immediately relieved of the treasure and prompted to go back in and get more. "Yeah, yeah, oh yeah," I heard the crowd of scientists and poohbahs exclaim. John was looking at me and smiling, and I knew he knew that we would be out of this pile of rocks and drinking Dom Pérignon champagne, always first class on the president's jet this very evening. One more thing to be done, however, was to lock up the "deal." I went back to Tut I and Tut II and told them what the greedy humans wanted. All the jewels! They knew that, and I said, "What if you could control the jewels, and thereby control them?" They said, "How?" I said, "Let's go!"

On my return trip into the tunnel, John knew what to do, and as he was appearing to adjust a bigger jacket on me, he also included some Coco Cabana Cha Cha cigars from the very heart of the Casbah. I introduced them to Tut I and Tut II. They took a blow and began to pontificate such as I had never heard before. Tut I would say this and that, and then Tut II would add more, and besides, and then again. The room was so full of smoke we had to move to another, which had even more jewels and gold, truckloads full. Before the place filled with smoke and their pontificating, I had to begin the plan. At the rate they were blowing smoke, actually and verbally, it would be no time at all before half the plan was complete. The plan laid out was this.

Make the pyramids and the surroundings invisible. While this is being done, all the loot will be moved to a place that only Tut I and Tut II know about. After seeing the diamonds, the greedy humans will surely tear down the pyramids to get to the rest, so it is necessary to move it all. In order to make the pyramid invisible, Tut I and Tut II will have to get all their friends together, maybe thousands. Create one of the legendary sandstorms that are so frequent in that area, only not just sand. You guessed it. A Coco Cabana Cha Cha cigar storm that will be caused by their friends puffing and snuffing until the whole thing cannot be seen. Under a cloak of invisibility, they will then transfer the wealth to a place of their choosing, and the rest will fall into place. (I feared at the rate Tut I and Tut II were blowing and going, they might make all of Egypt invisible. Boy, could those rats blow!)

I told them there just happened to be an ocean liner docked not too far away with one ton of these special cigars on board and would we like to make some kind of a trade. Laughter abounded as Tut I said, "You can have it all, just bring on the Coco Cabana and mix in lots of cha cha as well." Tut II was laughing uproariously and agreed with little pontificating as they could barely talk what with all the laughter and smoke going around. We decided they could have the entire shipment of cigars for a truckload of whatever I wanted. Okay, sounded fantastic!

They put ten more big diamonds in my cat care jacket, and I went back. Much oohing and ahhhing and flashbulbs were bursting as I was immediately relieved of the jewels. Since we were foreigners and because of the Egyptians great concern for animals, they decided to remove us immediately and place us on Air Force One, as the President's trip had luckily coincided with ours. As the wheels were encapsulated into Air Force One's wheel wells, we were encapsulated as well with much huzza huzza, more pictures, and of course, presidential champagne. (Dom, in case you want to know.)

We had just achieved our prescribed altitude when a smiling voice came over the intercom and said, "It appears we have just averted a tremendous sandstorm that will take some days to clear. All the people at the pyramid had to pull back to Cairo to wait until the storm lifts." All the papers in the world reported on the tremendous sandstorm that had made all the pyramids completely invisible. Since the storm was blowing toward Cairo, with a population of some ten million people, much of the storm ended there. It was reported that the huge storm had created confusion, as most of the population was outside going this way and that way with their arms in the air muttering some western nonsense. No injuries were reported, but many prayer towers were gone, and there was much talk about animal rights. Some cats were even seen being driven around in cars.

Ho hum…I hope I never have to go back there. In fact, I won't, not even for another truckload of stones. It turns out after the "storm" had lifted, one of the pyramids was torn down and nothing was found but a bunch of different animals and lots of smoke. Hmmmmm, you don't think? All in all, it was worth it. I did get my picture on the cover of *The Rolling Stone*, and that rock you see hanging around my neck will get me a whole lot of very tasty cat food. Meow! Makes me purrrrr…time for my catnap…zzzzzzzzzzzzz.

Irish Cooking

*M*usic is for the soul and food to help out with the rest of us, I thought, but John has come up with a new epicurean delight that mystifies me. Well, almost, lemons and garlic, and it isn't just made with a hint of lemon juice and a few sprinkles of garlic salt. I am meowing about a whole lemon and five or so cloves of garlic mixed in a blender with water. John says, "Grind it up and drink it and away you go!" Really! It works for John anyhow. He tried to get me to drink it, but of course, I just wagged my tail and gave him the "cat look." When he left and no one was looking, I took a nip and it was admittedly very good. Besides, it is proven that lemon and garlic help your digestive system and complexion. I guess even I will admit to vanity, wanting to gild the lily and make my fur and nails even more beautiful than what they are. (Just imagine my mink coat, as John calls it, being even more beautiful. Of course, my nails will be so strong I will be able to run up a rock wall. Can't wait to drink some more!)

One of John's friends was over to visit, and more BS led to more BS, and finally, John was about to burst. He told her he had a great culinary invention, and would she like to participate in a taste-testing session? "Sure!" she said. John went to the kitchen, put all the ingredients in the blender, and voila! A masterpiece! This time it consisted of six cloves of garlic, one whole lemon (rind and all), one bunch of green onions, one cup of water, and his special Irish blessing. When all was ready, he poured it into a chilled glass and presented her with the best thing, he told her, she would ever wrap her lips around. (Hmmm, I could not laugh now; I had to see what happened, so I saved it for later.) He told her he would like to know if she could tell him what the ingredients were while being blind-folded. She agreed. Since he does not have any silk napkins, he put a watch cap over her eyes and the taste-testing session began. She was positively joyous. (John, upon putting the concoction in the glass, also added some white lightning vodka, but it was the best.) She was all smiles, and immediately guessed the booze, and said, "This is some kind of a grapefruit drink."

"Good guess," John said. "You will get credit for one ingredient."

She kept smiling and in no time had finished the entire drink. She said it tasted great and could she now look. Sure. She had, in less than one minute, drank one lemon, rind and all, half a clove of raw garlic, four stalks of green onions, two shots of vodka, and six ounces of water, all properly chilled and professionally served, by all means. John then showed her what she had just drunk. She could not believe her eyes, her ears, her taste buds, or her nose, especially her nose. I, in the meanwhile, was on top of the kitchen ceiling chan-delier. As there was still a bit more in the blender, I did not want to wear any of it or become the next test subject. No thank you! She was great, and they laughed about it all. She was very charming and agreed that the immune capabilities and all-around wonders of the drink were fantastic. She then gave John the kind of smile I have seen in tigers' eyes while on safari with John when we were safe in a tour bus, and said, "But don't ever forget the vodka!"

New York, New York

"New York, New York," and so it goes as Sinatra sings. We are going to New York, and staying at the Waldorf Astoria with complete run of the house. Meow! The capital of the world! Now what? We are just going to be sightseers, look at this and that, and visit the oldest bar in America. George and Tom and John and Benjamin all had a snort or two in there. They were the absolute leaders of our country. We are still ruled by what they said. We were so lucky to have them. But, like winning football teams, you can't win every one, even though you are the best. Lately, America has had a lot of rotten leaders, more like liars, cheats, scammers, morons, creeps, jerks, slobs, and that's enough for now. But hey, we put them in, kind of, and...where was I? Time to head out the door and get on the plane, and off we went. So excited! I head-butted John a few times, and that was sure to get a laugh. He said, "You better watch your weight, Casey, or you could kill me, and then who would drive the car?" Really funny jokes all over the place. I jumped in the backpack and cat-batted John, and he laughed some more, and then into the taxi we went.

Soon we were on the plane in first class, me with my orange cat care jacket, stuffed full of pills to keep John going. He had taken himself down and got some kind of a suit that made him look like a professional quarterback and an international high roller.

Creepy, I thought, but what the hey? Soon, we were in the air over Phoenix in no time. They brought us whatever we wanted. Well, almost. I went to sleep under the backpack as John was looking out the window. I no sooner fell asleep thinking about Jefferson and Washington and Franklin than I got a tingle across my shoulders and down my spine. My cat sensor for trouble was giving me a call. I had to find out what it was. I knew approximately where the trouble was coming from, right across the aisle from where we were. A man and a woman, married looking, were extremely nervous and tense. I mind-melded with them and guess what. Yep, they were going to hijack the plane, happens all the time—but not with me and John aboard. I told John what was going on, and he said, "Watch this!" Oh, boy, I thought. When he gets going it is like watching the tigers in the zoo eat the food that is thrown into their cages with eleven-foot barge poles. They eat it quick and hard, like when they were back in the jungle, never knowing when they will eat again.

Along with his suit, John had brought a pair of Irish brogans that weighed about four pounds each, good walking shoes, or in this case, good cold-cocking shoes. I crawled out from under the backpack, meowed, and diverted the couple's attention. John got out of his seat, and in two seconds, one second for each moron, he punched each one in the chest with his four-pound shoe at a speed of about sixty miles per hour. One can only feel pain for about a second because the force immediately splits the heart and all arteries leading to it and then stops. So do you. John came over, sat down, put on his shoe, and growled a little. I love it! I may be housebroken, but I still know what my large cousins do. So exhilarating to see what they do happen in real life in front of my own blue eyes and whiskers. (My whiskers are almost like my eyes. They are sensors for all that goes on around me.)

The couple could not move and just sat there leaning against each other, looking like two married people sleeping peacefully. John put a couple of blankets over them, and then put some dark sunglasses on them as well. Perfect. When the stews came by, they did not want to wake them. For the entire trip they "slept," and no one was the wiser. Us, I mean. Meow!

We were the first ones off the plane, and that was great. We no sooner got into a taxi when we heard all kinds of police noise heading out to the airplane. Next day there was a big to-do on the front page of the *New York Times*. Two terrorists had been found dead wearing clothes that would detonate upon being triggered. Since they "died" from massive heart attacks, they were not able to activate the detonator. Truly, God must be on our side. Not the nutty Allah one; he is still in a well somewhere with his goats. Hummmmmmm…

Off to the Waldorf Astoria, Irish brogues and all, such great shoes. John had them shined in the hotel, and the Shine man said, "Beautiful shoes, and they are even broken in already." John winked, I mind-melded with the shine, and John said, "Yes, they are definitely Irish heartbreakers." Laughter so loud it even woke up some republicans watching the stock market reports in one of those stupid stock watching rooms. John said to the Shine, "Here's a Benjamin. You better go have a drink before you hurt something." Shine said, "Okay" and reached under the shine chair and pulled out a bottle of Stoli. Glasses were passed around, and it was a great but small celebration. I was sitting on the back of the chair with my paws on John's shoulder. The Shine looked into my cat eyes, and I told him this was between us three, blacks, whites, and cats. He said, "Ah do know what's you be talkin' about. I could feel something real tingly when I shined that one shoe. Daddy, I thought, this shoe be working real hard for such a young shoe." We all started to laugh again, and more Stoli was passed around. I even took a sip. The shoeshine man went on to tell us of his life. I could see it all in his mind, and I told John. He was eighty-five years old, still shining shoes, still drinking, and having a tremendous time. I could tell he, too, had some telepathic abilities. He had shined every shoe of almost everybody who was anybody in the world. Some camel jockeys had tipped him thousands, and he wanted to buy poison with it to kill them. But he carried on. "Doin' what a shine be doin'," he said. He and his wife, Kay Kay, lived in an apartment two blocks away. He said, "I probably have the best job in the world. I know what is going on all over the world because I can read a person by shining their shoes and tingling their feet. Their minds open up, and I can see everything as I can see your two minds now. John is a tiger in human form, and you, Casey, have a tiger inside you." John asked him whose shoes he had shined and what they were thinking. It was astounding. To put it simply, he knew it all. "Makes you want to cry," he said. "I talk to my wife, and she understands me, and we laugh a lot. She watches the Stoli, so everything is fine." We laughed, and I meowed. As he was talking to us, he found it necessary to shine John's shoes again. One never knows. In New York City's eight million people, one is never truly alone. We all agreed to stay in touch and help out if need be. The Shine, Willy, said, "I will need you twenty-four hours a day, but we can't do that, can we?"

John said, "We have tremendous power throughout the world, and really, nothing is beyond our ability. Just pick your options carefully. Otherwise I will have to buy Irish shoes by the dozen." We all laughed, and of course, I chimed in a little. We woke up a few more republicans and decided to call it a night. Meow!

Happy Cats

*H*appiness—that is secret of us cats. We are happy. Most folks do not know it. Since I am the rarest of rare, and with all my mental abilities, I am able to figure it out. When people see cats doing what cats do, there is always an element of small wonderment in their minds. What is that cat up to? Just simply being a cat, I must tell you.

At times I need a stimulant, and that is why I like to be around John, most of the time. But sometimes I do have to keep a keen cat eye on that guy, like today, for example. He is swimming again, and he wants me to come along. Meow to you, you old fox. I know you just want to get me in the Jacuzzi so you don't have to wipe me down with a wet towel once in a while. Although some cats love to swim, I, for one cat, am not crazy about it. Maybe I will go and jump in to make him happy, and then he might take me for a long car ride, listening to one of my favorite songs, "Crash, bam, alakazam over an orange-colored sky!" I call the singer "Cat" King Cole, such a great song. It was on the radio as I was lying on the dash, and I immediately became invigorated. John started singing the tune as I was cat-batting the air. We were ready for the stage. Music makes John and me.

Slow Boat to Hawaii

I'd like to take you on a slow boat to Hawaii. Meow! Meow! Have a boat! I have a boat! Every cat's dream in the whole world is to have a boat! Yeah, yeah, and double yeah! Of course, John will be the driver. John will pay the bills, do all the work, build a place for me to sleep, and do whatever has to be done to keep the boat afloat. But, yeah, yeah, I am the captain! Captain Casey! Has a pleasant ring to it, don't you think? I will read and decipher the astrological charts, shipping charts, time and wind changes, and most important of all, where we will go! I will be able to have my friends over and serve them any kind of food they want at any time, as long as it is in the ocean and I can catch it. I will always have the wind at my back, smooth seas ahead, and red sunsets in the evening! One more advantage that will make "our" boat invincible is that in the greatest cigar and cha cha deal ever, I obtained the alien cloaking device. If we run into the wave of all waves or impossible situations beyond belief, I will simply have the aliens beam me aboard by saying, "Beam me up! This is Catty! Boat, John, cigars, and Casey, altogether at once!"

After all, being a cat, our motto is "Live for today, and keep it going!" Don't take on a tiger with an ice-cream cone. I also know there are lots of hungry "things" in the great seas that will hunt me down forever when it has been discovered I am on their turf, ahem, waves. Believe me, evil lurks below, and I am their only true enemy. Somehow, they found out about tuna of the sea, and they think I am responsible for all the canned cat food in the world. Well, I'm not! I hate fish! I like lemons, baked potatoes, garlic, and onions. Fish food for me is phooey. My buddies can have all they want. For me, vodka over please, mixed in a ten-ounce glass of pureed lemon juice, rind and all. But I get the blame for all the canned cat crap. Everyday, evil below and above searches for me constantly, with vigor and hatred. They "know" I am the one that has kept them below, living and holding their breath in all that slimy seaweed. They are bitter, cold, and evil. With me gone, the world is theirs. Awkward at first, but with a good Jewish tailor and some speech lessons, they could pull it off. Lots of deodorant will help, and I do mean lots! Whatever comes along, I will be fully prepared for.

I have been dreaming of being on a boat all my life, and now my dream has come true! Before we leave tomorrow, I must contact Seagull Joe so at all times, every seagoing bird will be in communication with me if I want. To make them extra happy, I will tell them where the sardines hide. Cigars complimentary, of course. (I know that Uncle Al will now want to sell them mouthwash for all the junk they stuff in their bodies, too.) I must also have great water taxi service for all my friends. High above the deck is a fifty-foot catbird seat. Uncle Al will love it up there what with all the succulent scents and Havana Coco Cabana Cha Cha atmosphere. We must have a place of respite to think, plan, smile, meow, and always, but always, keep a sharp cat eye out for the evil ones!

Since the Coco Cabana Havana cigars made all this possible, we will also have a sufficient store of them for all occasions until the entire populace has puffed it up, smelled it, and saved itself from cancer. We must be ever vigilant to help whomever we can. For a good price of course—one hundred dollars for our specialty, Coco Cabana Cha Cha Cha Cancer Curing Cigars. Our motto for the cigar is "Why don't you pick me up and try me sometime?" It's an old seaman saying. It goes along with "When you start to puff, you can't seem to get enough." Now that all is shipshape, ahoy there, shiver me timbers, and blimey, as well. We will leave with the tide tomorrow. Sweet dreams to you. May you always have smooth seas, good luck, the wind at your back, and a smiling cat like me.

Music

I hear what people "call" music all the time. Huh?! Every cat can tell that is not music, but in most cases, some kind of pain being expressed vocally. To me, the sweetest, best music is that of a small kitten, so wonderful! Expresses all from Mozart, Beethoven, Sinatra, and that's enough for now. Why "they" bother repeating those horrible sounds is a loud, and I do mean loud, statement of human's inability to make pretty noises. After all, isn't that what music is? Of course! 'Nuff to make a cat laugh! Now, I rarely sing. When I was a kitten, I was so beautiful, both my singing and physically! Most cats are. Only Uncle Al can't even carry a Beatle sound, but we will cover Unk and his singing and much more later. Kittens sing so beautifully, with soulful expressions upon their faces, the range of their voices, the note variance and amplification. This mostly due to no smoking, as Sinatra will attest. What they sing about covers all that ever was, or will be, from food to love. After all, what else is there really?

Like I said, we can talk about Uncle Al and his "singing" later. But, just for now, please know that Uncle Al can do it all. He not only does the words and the melody, but he also mixes in every instrument that was ever invented, and lots that would be, if anyone ever heard Al singing one of his "melodies" from a place of his choice. Uncle Al sings from an excavated WWII bunker to the top of the Eiffel Tower. He likes to sing best when he is riding on seagulls, but has found out they either go 150 mph or dive. At times, and this is a concession, Al likes things smooth.

Many of my kitten cousins sing frequently and nicely, mostly about their mothers, food, and sleep. Beautiful words, phrases, and communicating sounds that only cats can do. It is so natural to us, and we enjoy it. But, enough is enough. Because I am an avid reader of Agatha Christie, Chandler Parker, Child, and many other "sleuths," I must refer to this particular cousin as the case of the singing kitten. She would not shut up. Her parents told me she had been watching TV, some show that had the Beatles, Johnny Cash, Sinatra, and other screaming types who were frequently on the Ed Sullivan Show. After watching the show, she began singing, not quite like a cat, but mixing in other Sinatra, Cash, Arnold, and what most would refer to as out-and-out screamers, trying to alleviate pain in their psyches, pain being the constant in all of the screamers. Well, cousin kitty let it all go, all at once, and luckily they were out in the top of the barn when she exploded in song. It drove all the cats away. The chickens, cows, and the rest of the farm animals left. It was way too much screaming for them. For three days and nights, she sang and sang and sang! Poor farmer had no idea what to do. None of them did. They finally called me, and I said, "Get away! She is going through her kitten phase!" Finally she quit, to everyone's great relief, smiled and meowed sweetly, but it was a close call. Ahhhh! Kittens singing like Sinatra and Presley would put a bounty on kittens' heads. We would all have to go and live with John and put up with his laughing at us and demanding payback. It would be a lot of fun though, I have to admit, with a laugh.

Sea Lions and San Francisco

I knew even at three days old something was coming to me mentally, indescribably. There I just described it—info from all over the cosmos. May I say, Einstein, Galileo (sounds like a cat's name), volatile aliens (yes, even them), and a total conglomerate of everything and every being who had had a thought or plan that would shape and understand all that is to be known or ever will be. Whew! Lots of stuff for a cat, but I didn't blink an eye. Well, maybe once. John could hear me think a little, and he went immediately to the fridge and had a cold one. I blinked a bit and meowed out loud, meaning, be quiet when I have a big thought coming in. Harrumph!

In addition to my own cat's consciousness, I also have a consciousness that monitors the first consciousness. One more consciousness is there, as well, but hardly ever has to do a thing—three in all. Too much for John. I heard him think, *I have a five-day-old cat thinking for all the world, and all I have to do is scratch his tummy to make him feel better. I mean, who is who here?* We were having great times, and now it was time to get serious and make the whole cosmos, the world, and the whole of whatever we ever can know and think about go the way cats would like it. I mean, really, aren't the cats the best!

John heard me say that, and I heard the fridge door opening. Then I jumped in his backpack and off we went for a walk around the bay area of San Francisco. Such a beautiful day! My whiskers were everywhere, picking up information 360 degrees up, down, and everywhere. I filtered what I wanted, and we continued to walk along the Embarcadero. We were hungry, we meaning me, and we went into the first place I suggested. John got wine and a spoonful of cheese and crackers. When the food arrived, he put the cheese and crackers in his pocket, and I was delighted. The waiter smiled, and hey, it's San Francisco, after all.

The next day at the advancing age of six days, more information came into my mind that was tremendously interesting. I had to use my third subconscious to get it all organized. My third subconscious said I was going to have to download some to you-know-who. It would be a good backup and besides, there was so much room there to put things that it would be entirely safe. I had to laugh, but I had a job to do. John immediately started to speak in quantum physics and multiplying numbers he learned in the third grade. I knew this was the perfect friendship.

That night, we—well, I should say I—became hungry. I wanted some food to eat, and I wanted it now. I suggested it to John, and off we went to the nearest Italian place in San Francisco. I was still small enough to be in his pocket. John got a piece of pizza and put it in the pocket where I was. Tasted okay, but real funky delivery. I made a note to give him some loud meows when he was sleeping peacefully. Then again, it would only make him smile and tug my tail. We were having a great time!

John and I had only been together a short while when I realized he was always trying to find the perfect diet drink. He finally decided upon a whole lemon and four cloves of garlic with a cup of water.

Put it in the blender, drink it immediately, and away you go, and it seems to be working. John absolutely loves garlic! Now he is trying to give me some. Okay, I don't like any kind of fish, so maybe this is what I need. I have noticed since he has been on the lemon garlic diet, he smells better. He smells like lemon and garlic.

So much we could be doing, but where to begin? Maybe just take care of the cruise ships that are coming and going out of San Francisco all the time. There is always some kind of a scandal. Most recently, we heard some of the cruise lines are importing drugs (you think?) and causing the kind of turmoil that drugs do. (I mean, by now, just let it go. If a person can't control what they put in their mouths, I don't know what to meow about.) The media says illicit dealers are making billions of dollars, and thousands of lives are being ruined by all the drugs.

I decided to look into the matter with Seagull Joe and Uncle Al. We got together on the roof by our chimney, which is one of the empowering points of the world, and discussed the matter. As usual Seagull Joe gave us the bird eye, Uncle Al was puffing on a cigar, and a couple of Al's protégés were in the background getting ready to give us the old heehaw because they saw us as fuddy-duddies. (Well, just for the record, one of the protégés would have fallen off the roof from laughing so hard at something Seagull Joe said, but was saved by the gutter that goes around the roof. So there! Now he has the moniker "guttercat" for a long time. Laugh at that, you bunch of know-it-alls. Harrumph.)

We decided to make it a simple plan. Use Al's brilliant protégés to get on board, get the drugs and the money. Seagull Joe and his "pilots" would swoop down and get it all, and that would be that. Seemed so easy. We planned to do the job the next night at midnight. Wanted to keep it simple for the brilliant protégées who thought we were fuddy-duddies. At midnight all was secure, and the drugs and the money had been found and carried off by Seagull Joe and his men. All the stuff was stored in a secure warehouse, and it looked like we had solved a major social problem. (A problem that could have been solved just as easily if people would quit jamming things in their bodies that should not be there.)

The next day was as quiet as Uncle Al after smoking too many Castro cigars. The city was shut down. No machines were moving. People had to walk everywhere. The restaurants, delis, and bars were doing a hand-over-fist business, and a few Irish marching bands started up. People were happy, getting exercise, drinking libations, and eating great food with epicurean delight. Smiles, clever repartee, and witty rejoinders were exchanged, and it certainly looked like we had performed a fantastic work of good. Could it be? Perfection? Happiness without all the falderal of stupid drugs and money and morons making it all a bigger mess. I moved my tongue across my whiskers and realized I had been taking a "catnap." Droplets of water were covering me and the rest of the group. Apparently, Uncle Al had puffed it up too much. What with that and the chimney smoke, the beauty of the night, the sea breeze blowing by our eyes and mind, we had taken a brief siesta. Even the protégées were off to the side sleeping on their backs and waving their paws in a cat dream. (Wish I had a picture of that to show those young whippersnappers.) We all hurried back to our dry and safe homes.

In the morning, front page, two-inch headlines of the *San Francisco Chronicle* read: "Strange flotsam and jetsam floating all around cruise ships! Sea lions were swimming around in the stuff and barking loud enough to be heard all over town. Some had come on shore and demanded pizza from delis." (They were polite, the paper reported, but a bit loud.)

Apparently, we had not invited a representation of sea lions to our meeting, and they decided to look into the matter themselves. All was smoothed over. The head of the sea lions, aging Charlie, said he was sleeping peacefully under Pier 49 when the entire racket began. Some drug types were coming off the cruise ship in the middle of the night with large black bags that looked like baby sea lions. ("Poor vision, you know," Charlie said.) The young sea lions, trying to be heroic, shoved all in the bay. The bags weren't baby sea lions. They were full of Bahama Momma Ganja. All the dope fell into the water, looking like seaweed at midnight, and some thought it was *Breakfast at Tiffany's*. (Some sea lions saw the movie once, and told everyone it was their turn now.) We all agreed we had done the right thing, especially the sea lions. They were so sick of octopus that it was great to break up the monotony. Pizza bills were paid for by the SPCA.

Hollywood?

*P*uss in Boots*! Great show, and I loved it! The star of the show reminded me of me. It's always nice to see the cat world get some publicity. Pure Hollywood, however… I never heard a cat say one word of any human language. We have evolved way beyond all that gobbledygook and confusion that apparently 500 different languages on this planet cause. No matter where a cat goes, he can speak immediately to any other cats succinctly.

One thing cats also have in common with humans is that there are some very, very nasty cats all around that will kill and eat you. At least most humans only kill each other. I know Hollywood would have you think otherwise, and that is another reason I won't go to Hollywood. John is always thinking about doing something with me to make me. Every now and then when I read his mind, he has us both in a scene where I am sitting on his shoulder, and he is giving orders to James Bond, the original James Bond. John is younger than Sean Connery, so already the scene is cat and weapons. Then he wants to boss me and James Bond around and have me go "Meow, Meow," and act like an airhead cat. Too much for me! It will never work. Why? Because I am too smart.

Maybe I should tell crazy Uncle Al about the part and see if he will take it. What, am I kidding?! Uncle Al would jump a crow and be there in a half hour. He would give cats a bad name in a hurry. Then again, crazy Al's idea of a good time would inspire writers for monster movies for years to come. The vampire cat of Paris! The cat who ate whatever! Cats without remorse! Crazy cats who do voodoo! Cats who turn into humans! The pope is a cat! You get the message... Meow!

I Wanna Be in Pictures

*T*V is good for cats. We hardly ever actually watch it. We just use it to hone our cat stare, which people find so mysterious and inscrutable. Uncle Al was visiting, and we were working on our mysterious stares when Al actually started paying attention and said to me, "What is that, and what are they doing?" I knew immediately that Al's brain had begun to click, and a plan was formulating in his effervescent subconscious cat mind. I gave him a brief sketch of movie generalities and explained that you really don't see what you think you see. You only see what they want you to see. Al, never being one to couch his questions in drawn-out blather, simply said, "How can I make a movie? I know I can do it, and I can do a better job than what I have just seen, and maybe make enough money to get John the Bentley he is always dreaming about." Much meowing, purring, and tail wagging ensued, and in about one minute Al had it all figured out. He would be the director, actor, producer, writer, and whatever else it took except for one thing: neither of us could drive a car to get the equipment to go to Hollywood in order to begin. I told him a movie could be made anywhere; it is actually a big fake on our imagination, and the term "Hollywood" is really only synonymous with all the falderal that goes into making movies, on and off the set, present and past and what will be.

Al cat-batted the air with his beautiful, anxious paws at a great rate of speed. He stood up and walked around the room on his hind feet while waving the air with one paw and gesturing with some kind of a baton in the other, and proclaimed with eyes aglow, "We're going to make a movie, be famous cats, get John a Bentley, and let the chips fall where they may." *And, not in that order*, I thought, and had to excuse myself while I went outside so no one could hear me. I had a big fat cat laugh, albeit respectful, for about two minutes. When I returned, Al had much of the details thought through. All he needed was a high-powered movie camera, some Sinatra music, a makeup crew, and as the movie "progressed," he would get what he needed.

Then Al went on to say he had wanted to make a car such that a cat could drive it, but it would have to wait until the movie was complete and distributed. Yes, he had already figured out distribution and knew who he would get to do it. I was so relieved. Then he said it would be seagulls and pigeons. I had to excuse myself again. I got John to get the camera, and he rented a huge barn in the country, and away we went. John had some idea something was up, and when Al showed up dressed like Jackie Gleason, in one of his Hollywood directing skits, John knew the game was afoot. John immediately took the camera into the barn, started smoking a cigar, and had a glass of Dom Pérignon. All of us gathered in the barn and by now, Al was wearing some kind of a French lid and smoking a cigarette with a one-foot holder and drinking some of John's champagne in a small glass. He hopped up on a table and said this was going to be the greatest, purely artistic movie ever made. He said he was the director, but that we could all take turns, and not to let our inhibition or lack of a German accent get in the way. We then all smoked big cigars, drank champagne, and readied, er, steadied ourselves for what would soon be the greatest movie ever made.

By now the barn was filled with hundreds of different kinds of animals, and then Al brought in the makeup crews. All the animals lined up quickly and were dressed, given haircuts, had more hair put on, given various types of tools and machines, and given instructions from many directors who came from seemingly nowhere. The whole thing seemed to come from nowhere, yet everyone and everything were working in perfect harmony.

I even found myself in a line where I was given devices and clothes and instructed about hundreds of different things to do, and when to do them. In ten minutes, Al was ready, and a large raccoon from the top of the barn swinging on a rope yelled, "Stations!" Al meowed loudly, "Action!" and away we went. There was no hesitation, no stops and starts, no complications, missed lines, questions, breakdowns, or a smidgeon of something that would break and not help create the making of the greatest movie the world will ever see or know about. The movie began where all time began, and brought in every nuance and thing and person and living being that had ever been around at that specific period of time. The movie would continue to where you are reading these very words.

There was consummate action all over at once. The filming never stopped, and the actors, directors, and hundreds of the other crews all went along with one filming twenty-four hours a day. Music, laughter, sorrow, lightning, love, wars, catastrophic physical causes from everywhere in the cosmos were given detailed attention, coverage, and scientific interpretation. Whatever was happening, or happened, by any living entity was filmed, noted, and brought to the viewer's attention in such a way as each could understand with their own ability. As the movie progressed, more and more people, animals and things and helpers appeared and kept the filming moving along at a scintillating, joyous, humorous, scientific, artistic, and comprehensible pace. On and on the moviemaking went for fourteen nonstop days. It had covered everything and everyone any-body could imagine, prove, think of, relate to, talk about, or pay for that had happened since the beginning of time. Truly, this was the greatest movie ever made!

We had so much film after two solid weeks of making a movie that we had to figure out a way to make it practical, so one could sit to show the movie anywhere and anytime with as little fuss and bother as possible. Problem solved! For the last two weeks, I had noticed about ten rats playing cards in the corner of the barn. They were dressed like scientists, spoke in different languages, and I could not believe my cat eyes to see them cheating each other con-stantly. When one went to the bathroom or made a call, they would switch his cards around and pretend nothing had happened. They were smoking so much that a small fire broke out, and one rat stole all the money. They continued as if normal, and I knew immediately they were brilliant rats and could do anything.

Sure enough, three rats walked over and said we should con-solidate all the film into a very small object that everyone in the world could use. They said they knew how to do it, and did we want it done. Of course we did, and within two days all the movies were consolidated into an object that could be used by everyone in the world, anywhere, with no expense other than the initial sale. Payment was discussed as to how much the rats would charge, and I said, "Name your fee." The rats did not know that I could read minds and foresee the future. It stands to reason from what I saw the rats do to each other that they were ready for anything. The rats' fee was something only a scientific rat who attempted to swipe the linear accelerator from Stanford would charge. I said, "I will triple the fee if I can't guess what the object is, and if I do, it will be free." The rats immediately laughed and squealed as rats do, and spoke to me in Chinese. They said, "We want all the cigars and champagne we can drink until we die as well." I spoke in cat, I meowed, and said, "Deal!" We shook paws and tails and stuff, and then came the moment of a rat payment, and free cigars and champagne until they died. I said, "The object you have invented that will give everyone in the world complete access to this great movie is a hollowed-out penny. Because of modern technology, it was made possible, and we know all about it." The rats, Mike, Ike, and Ramona, said, "Rats!" (a given) and many other unprintable things, but held to their word, and the deal was done. We still threw in the cigars and champagne, the barn and the swinging raccoon. A Bentley pulled up with John driving and smiling. All the cats and rats jumped in and immediately began beating each other at cards. After all, with cards, cigars, booze, and a Bentley for life, who cares about another stupid movie?

Don't Be Catty

*I*t seems like that is what is happening to America. A person can't say a thing without catching all kinds of phooey. Only certain people can say certain things that nobody else can say. Say whatever, but you better be in the group that can run their gums, and have carte blanche in doing so. This is not at all like the cat world. We speak all the time, at once, about everything, in different languages, every nanosecond of the day, for as long as we were here. Not humans— wrong thing said and hello walls. (Loved that song, "Hello Walls"... Oops, gotta get back.) Here we are. No matter what country, free-dom of speech is all right if you can back it up with lots of money or bullets or ideally both. For example, you go to work tomorrow and start saying "stuff," and you will get in trouble. This will become evident in the following ways: like somebody squealing on you, get-ting in your face, displaying their numerical IQ, or maybe so far as the gray bar hotel. How come? Rhetorical question and we all know the answer, and the answer is this has turned into George Orwell's *1984*. Answer is also sung about by the Kingston trio, "Tiny Boxes." (Absolutely my favorite group of singers; Sinatra can't be my fave any longer.)

We, the world, have placed ourselves in a cooking pot with lots of water, olive oil, and salt, and we are beginning to simmer, and soon we will go whoooooosh! Like Uncle Al sounds when he takes off on his favorite seagull taxi ride, Al and his taxi service and oth-er people who relate to that type of wherewithal will be the only ones left. What then? More rhetorical stuff, we start all over again. (Another great song by a great singer.)

It can be stopped at any time. If we throw out all of the religious claptrap and do the job. (I know you're saying that is just what a cat would say, and you're right. Do the job!) Cats are about 99 percent sane on our aggregate. Fifty percent of humans are completely nuts, and all but about 1 percent has a brain that is completely functional and not poisoned by that religioso stuff. We shoot, choke, bury, bomb, stab, poison, and fill in the blank_____ for what we do to each other, all the time since the beginning of time. A world led by dopes, creeps, diabolical, witless morons, and I would have you fill in some more blanks, but I would run out of ink.

You want examples. Look anywhere. Look at your hands. What is everybody doing with their hands? Weird things—painting, cutting, sewing, scrapping, chewing, rubbing, smelling, crabbing, and enough already. Look some more and what do you see? TV, you say? (Don't tempt me! And what does that mean by the way? Sorry, gotta move on.) So, now you are thinking about leadership in the world that often is incarcerated by laws they are upholding. Or, maybe the biggest question of all, my gawd, even bigger than TV and Hollywood, is why do we fight constantly, all over the planet, and it never stops? We kill each other, eat each other, cheat each other, poison each other.

Only now, it finally takes a cat, me the guy in the beautiful mink coat, with the beautiful whiskers and quicker hands than Manny Pacquiao, to tell you what is going on in your mind! By now, my dear reader, you must have realized, this is one smart cat! Oh, yeah! Aha, the cat is out of the bag! You now are privileged to know that I am the greatest reader of minds, the best reader of the future and mind-melder manipulator that the world has ever known. There are only a couple of us from the millions of cats born that have my ability, about one per century. I am the chosen one at this moment. I am not worried about "going away," because there will always be another one after me to help out the world. Or, like the James Bond show *Moonraker*, "you better get on board." (Hmmm, another good song.) I have no ego, but I know exactly what must be done, and I am gratified to know there are lots of people who agree with me. Have to laugh and meow real loud now! Although Uncle Al is one of my best friends, he agrees with me not one iota. He is a great cat and means well with every paw he uses to steal candy bars, but he will fight at the drop of a whisker, and if you told him he would be bishop of Baltimore, he would break his tail on a seagull getting there in time. Whatta nut!

We cannot do a thing about our peculiar condition. Hope you are on the right side or fight. If you don't kill them, they will kill you, guaranteed. You heard it here first, and if shocked, you are a dummy, unintelligent, uninformed, lowlife entity, or you just don't care about your life and those around you. Another movie comes to mind and it is aptly named: *It's a Mad, Mad, Mad World*. Title is perfect, but the content is pure Hollywood nonsense. The people working and acting in that movie were great, but they dared not touch upon the biggest truth in the world. Could it be the entire country while seeing that movie knew subconsciously that the world was completely messed up but went along with the happy Doris Day face because to admit with total consciousness that we were all mad would demand driving Budweiser and Guinness out of business forever? One drink at a time; one drink at a time. These words of wisdom are as responsible for keeping the world afloat as "God save the queen," "Allah lives in a well," "God is good," "Praise the Lord," "Pass the ammunition," and all other kinds of claptrap sayings that one hears every day.

I will say out loud what I really feel, and I can do it because I am a cat. Humans are goofy and evil. If you know this to be true, be quiet. If you don't believe it, you will probably light a candle, grease up your gun, get drunk, get in a fight, raise your blood pressure, call your mom (if you are lucky enough to have one), squeal and cause problems wherever you can, or what the heck? If you were that way, you would not be reading what a cat has to say. "It's you and me against the world, brudder." (A great Carly Simon song.) Also, as Al and I are up here on our favorite chimney overlooking the great city of San Francisco, I have to leave you with a song by the great Antonio Benedetti. He sings it, and he can back it up. "If I Ruled the World." Meow!

It's Good to Be a Cat

No doubt about it, cats have it all. In my particular case, I have so much more that sometimes I think I know how humans must feel when they get greedy. Good thing that I have it and not a human, or they would not know what to do with all these skills, and more than likely would make a mess of it. You don't have to go too far to see what people do with tremendous abilities in one way or another and do preposterous things in so many different ways. All you have to do is when you go grocery shopping is look at the magazines and see what horrible problems people get themselves into.

All I need is a modicum of comfort—food, quiet, and a ray of sun is a bonus—and I am what I am. A cat. Just to sit down and wrap myself in a furry ball with my tail around my body, to the left or right, and I am in cat heaven. For entertainment I can always tune in to the various minds around me or take a quick peek into various parts of the future, and that is fine with me. The world will go on. Cats will continue to watch and curl up, and people will act like some of my young relations, the kittens, do.

For a brief time in a cat's life, we act like we have no brains (or the brains we have are completely off balance). My kitten cousins are to be avoided. I took one look inside their minds, and I left immediately. One wanted to fly (it had just seen a bird), and it tried to fly immediately. It crawled up a tree, went out on a limb, and jumped and waved its paws as hard as it could, for as long as it could, and then landed in a grass patch. It tried again and again. Another one was fascinated with the vacuum and the noise it made, and wanted to somehow control it or command it to do what it wanted. It attacked the vacuum constantly when it was used and loved every second of it. It kept a close eye on the closet the vacuum was in and for three days did not move from under the couch, waiting for the vacuum to come out again. All the trouble they caused for doing silly, crazy things that were impossible, without logic, and could never possibly be achieved were exact blueprints that humans do every day everywhere.

Another one of my kitten cousins became fascinated with feathers and could not get enough of them. (Sound familiar?) She searched continually and everywhere for feathers, never eating, sleeping, or stopping for a second. It was the holiday time of the year, and you guessed it. The family got a turkey and decided to do everything from scratch. During the night, although the turkey was on top of the fridge, the small kitten managed to drag it into the living room and completely "undressed" it. It certainly gave the family a head start on dressing the turkey, but so much was a hopeless mess. In the morning they found the kitten asleep on a pile of messed-up feathers with a cat smile on her face and feathers sticking all over her body. I did not follow up on what happened. I did not want to. I have no desire to do what newspapers do all over America and that is to report all the silly, crazy happenings that go on. Why? It sells papers, you say. Okay, back to curling up in a ball and waiting for John to take me for a ride, and getting a glimpse of his mind which is so reminiscent of the kitten I now call Turkey.

Lucky for John, I can influence him and get him to think more like a cat. I have saved him from so many stupid things that I can't count them all. Well, I can, but why bother. Why do I do it? I know the answer to my own question, as well, but there are more important things to do, which reminds me, time to curl up and get this cat show on the road.

B'gosh and B'gora, the Irish Are Here!

ime to kiss the Blarney Stone, I'm afraid. John wants to go back to his roots and look up some of his long lost relations. He says the Irish love cats, alive only. I can't say as much for lots of other places. When we arrived in Dublin, it was a sparkling day. Into the backpack I went, and then into a cab with John. The cabbie took one look at me in the backpack and said, "Sweet Mother Mary, Holy Jesus, and the saints preserve us," and started laughing. He asked John about me, and did the blarney begin to fly. We hadn't even kissed the great stone. He told the cabbie that I was his care cat, specifically. John said, "Casey, here, not only carries life-giving pills with him at all times, but he is also my four-leaf clover. Everyone loves Simon, and when I play cards with him, I never lose."

"How can that be? If it's true, I will buy him from you and quit driving people like you around."

Much laughter ensued. I knew this guy had kissed the great stone, and I wondered if there was any stone left after his visit. John said, "I'd be glad to sell you Casey. I can guarantee if you play cards with him, you will never lose, but there is one catch." (Isn't there always?) "No matter how much you bet or win, it is very difficult to collect your money."

The cabbie asked, "Why?"

John said, "Because Casey cheats like crazy and never pays his debts. Why just the other day…"

The cabbie began laughing until he got his whiskers wet, and said that this trip was on him. He took us to the best place in Dublin where we could meet and relax with the good, and the great, and the not so great. John gave him eighty dollars when we arrived, and I hammed it up by meowing outrageously and cat-batting John on the shoulders, and much more laughter ensued. The cabbie then told all the folks there that we were one of them, and to watch out for us and give us anything we wanted. "Just don't wake them for a weekday mass, and don't gamble or drink with the cat." I knew I was going to have a lot of fun.

We went into the most beautiful lounge in all of Ireland. We were received like royalty, although it is said the Irish hate royalty, but they know how to be, act, and treat one royally. (More about the Irish logic later, much, much later, in fact.) Bushmills and Guinness ruled the evening. It was known to all that I could go anywhere and do anything I wanted. The barman looked at John pleadingly, and John said, "Don't worry. He knows exactly what to do. His only weakness is cheating at cards, and even then, he is rarely caught. Doesn't it remind you a lot of royalty?" Laughter all around since I was walking up and down the one-hundred-foot round bar in the middle of the lounge, with a meow here, and a meow there, with my tail waving back and forth, and never touching a person or a thing. However, when I would come within a scintilla of doing so, the patrons were completely charmed. Only when passing by a particularly interesting lady did I give a soft meow and cat-bat the air once or twice. Business was quadrupled we were told, and it was due all to us, and so now, everything was on the house! As the evening progressed, so did we. By this time, word had spread that we (I can say "we" since we are in Dublin) had discovered the Coco Cabana

Cha Cha Cha Cancer Curing Cigar. (In doing so, and in dealing with Castro, we let all know that we left him with nothing but his beard and bad breath. Boy, he was a stinker!) Cigars were passed out to all, and it was decided by the powers that be (yes, I did place a small suggestion in their minds) that this great chain of international hotels would sell nothing but Cha Cha Cha's. They would also install in every hotel a special Cha Cha Cha Cigar Room. All were happy and went home with Bushmills and Cha Cha breath.

The next day, it was time for the Blarney Stone, more Irish food, Bushmills and coffee, maybe a horse ride, and would you believe, to watch the moon come up on Galway Bay? It was too much, so we decided to go back home before all the blarney and Bushmills and every other word that starts with a "B" in Ireland wore us out completely. Ah yes, the Irish! Indefatigable, humorous, cantankerous, loving, brilliant, and watch out! Now that they are free from cancer, they may live forever! B'gosh and B'gora!

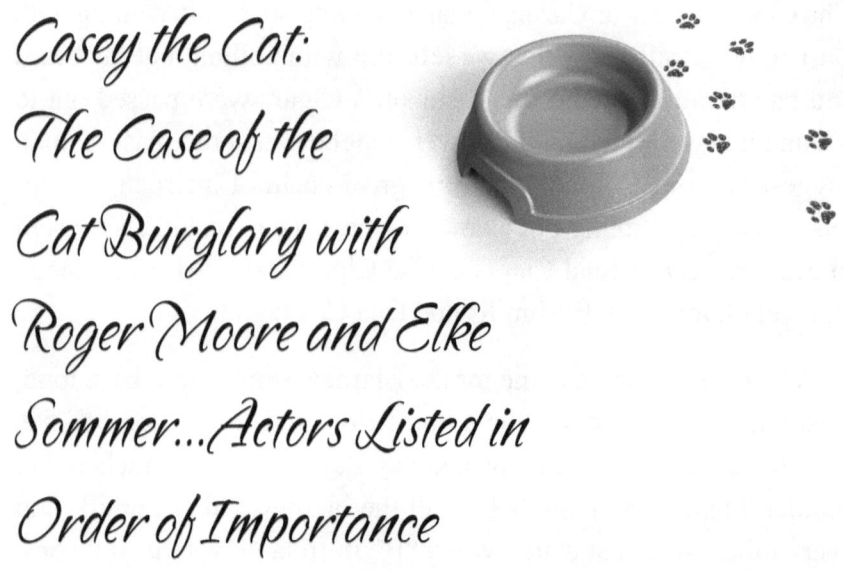

Casey the Cat: The Case of the Cat Burglary with Roger Moore and Elke Sommer...Actors Listed in Order of Importance

One of the best TV movies I have ever seen is *The Saint,* starring Roger Moore, later of James Bond fame. John and I would never miss a show, and we both laughed and meowed like crazy. The Saint reminded me so much of me. Suave, debonair (I don't like the oft misuse of the word, but it definitely is me), sophisticated, wealthy, good-looking, and if he had my eyes, he would have been better-looking than I am. All those great shows done with all those great pictures of London when you could still get a camera in London and do some excellent film work with a modicum of falderal. One movie reminded me so much of some of the things I have done, I almost thought they had a profile on me. Let me tell you how it all begins.

It was a foggy day in London Town. (How could I not use that for an opener?) The Saint really could have been me. He was dressed in his exquisite suit, as I am always in mine, and he was pursuing the chief of the KGB in London. It was an impossible job, but the Saint had to catch the agent or the world would surely come to an end. About halfway through the movie, a cat appeared in one of the scenes, and it certainly caught my attention. The cat continued to be in every scene thereafter. I am very sure it was Me Dear Mither. So beautiful, demure, she carried herself with aplomb and surety. She purred and meowed on cue and wonderfully well, I might add. They had dressed her in a diamond necklace, and it set off her sparkling blue eyes as well as any cat eyes that have ever been shown on the big screen. After all, these were the actual diamonds of the Great Russian Empire and valued at one hundred thousand pounds. (That is now the cost of a condo in Palm Springs, and then, the cost for the whole floor on the Waldorf Astoria in New York City.) Scene after scene came and went, and Roger Moore caught the KGB agent, Zero Mostel, and then ended up in the welcoming arms of Elke Sommer. Even for a cat, I was very attracted, well, somewhat mentally and emotionally, to that beautiful woman. (She walked like a cat, don't you think?) There was a gala party with Elke and Roger, and can you imagine two more beautiful actors? (I know what John will say, so I won't ask him. My whiskers are still sore from laughing about the Harry Truman joke. Guess you had to be there.)

My mother was said to have been there as well. She was named Florence, and behaved like a Florence. She did everything on time, purred on command, and meowed with grace and timing. It was even rumored that she spent the nights of the filming with Elke and Roger, and that later on, she became the live-in cat, if there is such a thing, of the great Elke. As I was born into a somewhat luxurious household with excellent cat facilities and silk sleeping beds, I have often wondered how it came about that I was born and lived in such a place. (Compared to my brethren, most of whom were born on the prairies and great cities of our world, it was a very different lifestyle indeed, and it fit me well. Ahem.) Upon doing some research with the same computer as I am writing this adventure on, I found that at the exact time of Me Dear Mither's acting stint, there was a scandal, almost as bad as the one in Bohemia, about the Czar of Russia's stolen great white cat necklace. If I may say, and I will, the plot began to thicken. It also coincided with both the careers of Roger Moore and Elke Sommer and the huge oceangoing yacht they acquired shortly after the movie *The Saint*. Also, it seems that the luxuriously beautiful cat in the final eight scenes of the movie was never seen again, and neither have the jewels. Do you think? "Meow!" I say to you. Then again, the purr doesn't fall far from the tree.

Caturday

eautiful day today! My silver and black-tipped fur is shining, my whiskers are white and bright, and I saw two treats for breakfast in the fridge this morning. Apparently, John did Chinese food last night. As usual I went into the fridge to look around. Voila! Chinese food, and I ate it all. John will wonder and then he will look at me and smile. John is getting to look like a cat more and more. At least his whiskers are white, and so is his hair. He will look like an old cat if he evolves, wily and smiley.

While watching TV, I have to laugh at all the nonsense I see. Albeit briefly. Some football player has perpetuated a hook that has captured the imagination of the entire media world. Maybe even in China, where they imitate my smile. It seems he has been telling human interest stories of deaths in his family and his girlfriend's as well. I find no personal interest, but I had a cat laugh at all the energy that has been expended by all that cat litter.

As if the human race doesn't have enough things to do already. Think of all the baths they could give us cats. All the Chinese dinners, all the rubdowns, car rides, catnip and accolades, and kitty kitty talk they could do. Maybe even take the dog, Rufus, for a walk, or better yet, take pictures of crazy Uncle Al catching a ride on a seagull going to San Francisco for the opening of anchovy season.

I was watching the history channel, my favorite, and it showed what we cats were doing five million years ago. Eating each other mainly, and chasing down toady things for snacks. Forget it! Give me John's fridge and the wine he leaves in his glass when he falls asleep watching TV. Now that's living!

Las Vegas

*W*e only live one hundred miles from Vegas. Since we live close, I can say Vegas. John said we must go to Vegas because a love of his life was singing there, the lovely Miss Joanie Collins. Guess he can't get that fabulous record jacket out of his brain where she sat cross-legged, naked, and stared stoned at fifteen million people who bought the album. Ho hum! So, off we went. We got there in plenty of time so John could take a nap and be fresh for Joanie. Big "Meow," I say. There was a huge ceiling mirror over the bed, and that alone was worth the trip. I lay down also, and looked at myself as I had never done before. Beautiful, just beautiful, looking at myself this way. I moved this way and that while looking at myself in the mirror, and thought, *No wonder everybody says I am so good-looking; just look at me!* My self-admiring ended when John rolled over and grabbed my tail, gently holding on to it. He considers it good luck, so I had to stay still for about half an hour. Even cats have it rough sometimes.

The show was at nine, so we went down two hours early. John even shaved and would have put me in the tub, but I escaped with a warm cloth wash. By this time, I was thinking of moving out and living on the roof by the chimney, but really, I was enjoying every second. First, the mirror on the ceiling, and then John cleaned me, saving me the effort, and now, ladies and gentlemen, the great, the one and only, Joanie Collins! Huzza, huzza, and throw in a meow or two as well. Yes, it was going to be a great night just watching how John would react to Joanie.

One would have thought that he was getting to return punts like he did when he played football. Very nervous, kept snorting, and slapping himself, and I had to go under the chair so he wouldn't see me laugh. So much fun, watching him carry on, ranting like this.

On the way down, standing up in the backpack with my paws on John's shoulders, moving my head from side to side while twitching my whiskers, I felt the hair on my neck stand up, and I naturally put my ears back. (What was I doing, I thought, returning to the Stone Age?) I felt danger, a tingling evil lurking here. Something no good was going on in that place. I became even more observant as we entered the lobby area and prepared to see the show. All of a sudden I heard lots of yelling, then gunshots. Aha! The game was afoot. We immediately lay down behind one of the slot machines and tried to look like the rug. I got out of the backpack and went to see what was going on while John was still trying to look like the floor. Good boy! There were four men yelling at everyone. They were wearing cat masks and waving their guns around. (At least they were doing something right.) They were pushing a huge cart with a big bag on top that everyone thought was stuffed with money. It wasn't money at all, and you guessed it. It was John's Joanie! (Oh, my little cat heart! John would be so upset!)

I climbed up on a structure that was about ten feet high, and I was able to get a quick read as to what they were doing. They were kidnapping Joanie because they were madly in love with her, and I do mean madly crazed. Like John, they could not get over that look of her on the album cover. All John did was shave and bath me, but oh no, these mad, crazed men had to take her. As they were pushing the cart to the elevator door, I did what every cat does naturally. I walked between their legs and tripped the first two, lickety-split cat finesse. The next two tripped over them to complete my cat judo job. They fired off a few shots into the ceiling as they fell. The cart continued into the open elevator, and voila, John pushed our floor button. It seems he knew he could not be a carpet for long, so while crawling around he decided to get in an elevator and leave. Wouldn't you know it? Now, he was with me again and, of course, Joanie. I thought that was a heck of a way to use your luck, but I never claim to understand people.

We immediately went to our floor and pushed the cart into the room. Now what? At that moment I made a slight suggestion to Joan—I was calling her Joan already—that we were her saviors and not her captors. John unzipped the bag, smiled his best Chinese cat smile, and helped her off the cart. She was all shook up (I guess when one goes to Vegas, one slips into its vernacular by osmosis). She sat down, John brought her some champagne from those well-stocked fridges they have to calm her down a little, and I got on the bed to survey what would happen next. Now I could not only see myself, but also Joanie and John. The cat's meow, I would have to say. While she was calming down, she spoke about how she was kidnapped, and thanked us profusely for saving what surely was her life. She called in to her manager agent, and said all was okay, that she had gotten away safely, and she would call back when things had settled down. When you are Joanie Collins, you do what you want. Hmmm, it seems like I am always running into cat people.

Joanie and John continued to talk about this and that, and the champagne was flowing. John said he just happened to have some special cigars from Havana and would she like a puff or two? He told her the complete story, almost, of the world-famous Coco Cabana Cha Cha Cha Cancer Curing Cigar. Since Joanie was one of the original hippies and had many causes célèbres, she was completely ecstatic with the cigar and, as it turns out, with me as well. Huh? She also told us she is on the animal bill of rights movement, and cats happened to be her favorite animal. Well, I don't consider myself exactly an animal. I am a cat. I rolled around on the bed, cat-batted the air a bit, and waved my tail with reckless abandon. Joanie was simply agog! She immediately came over, picked me up, and said I was a coochie, coochie, coo, and do you want to come home with me? In holding me, my whiskers touched her face, and I got a complete read of her mind. She now wanted me for herself, and she was willing to pay John millions of dollars in order to have me because I was truly one special cat. I knew that, but no, it would not be considered. (She was going through a phase that one has after being kidnapped. They know their life has been reclaimed, and from then on they want to do whatever they want and live life to the fullest. Sometimes that enthusiasm can bump back with quite a thud.) She immediately told John that she wanted me and simply had to have me. After all, she could tell that John was not exactly, shall we say, a George Clooney, and even on a good day, he would be hard-pressed to be a Mickey Rooney. Also, John was so excited to see her that in his haste to see the act, he had put his shirt on inside out. (Now you blew it, pal, I thought.) She went on to say she would be willing to pay handsomely for me and to just name his price. Immediately, all the champagne he had just drunk, and all the years of thinking about her on the album cover, disappeared. He smiled and said with some sadness, "Could you just sing a couple of verses from the song 'Someday Soon'?" She said sure, and she did. It was wonderful. Some "water" got on both John's and my whiskers, and she said she had to go to the ladies' room.

For all we know (see what I told you, there goes another song title), she may still be in the ladies' room. I quickly jumped in the backpack faster than I had ever moved before, and we were heading out of Vegas in two minutes flat. As I looked in the rearview mirror, I caught a glimpse of John's eyes. They reminded me of the eyes of the big tigers we saw on a safari trip, and it sent a chill up my mink-covered, mind-reading, mental telepathy self. Loved it! And to think, he got me for just a song. Meow!

Hitchin' a Ride

I got bored all of a sudden, and I decided it was time to go for a ride and look around. I told John, and off we went. John wasn't sure where to go, so I "suggested" Wal-Mart, like I "suggested" going for a ride, and off we went. I am crazy about Wal-Mart. First of all, John has to ride around in one of those motorized carts, and he puts me in the front basket. Wonderful! Whatever I want I get. John always needs something, so it fits in perfectly. Today John was getting some kind of pills for his back and just wanted to smell the meat in the deli. John almost bought a chicken but at the last second "changed" his mind. It would take us a month to eat it and yucko! A few people commented to John about me, and he told them I was his care cat, and that it was an evolutionary movement. Good job, John. People were impressed, and then a clerk came up, and John told him more baloney. I can't control everything. Well, I can, but I just do the big stuff.

John got a book by Lee Child, so interesting and well written. He will read the book and never pay attention to me, and then I have to do all the work around the house, which takes about two minutes. I read the books as well, and I hope John is reading mine. His plots could use a cat like me. I know everything. I am beautiful and intelligent beyond description, and I have John to take care of the money. What else! Oh, I know there is so much more, but I like to keep it simple. Don't want to overload John number one, and number two, when we signed up for this trip, there were no guarantees. (I better watch it or I might break off into some kind of a philosophical re-port. I like action, just get the job done, and keep the show moving. Philosophy is just that. Russia is all philosophy and, oops, I slipped up a bit there. Moving on.)

John has high blood pressure. He knows how good I am for him and that's why he puts up with a loud "Meow!" now and then. Today it was 140 over 83. Tonight it will be much lower. I almost have the answer, but for the present it is too complicated to explain. I am working on him as well as I can, and I am completely confident that his condition will be going away, and then he can take me to Paris. I will love it there. He might. But as long as there is champagne, he will be happy, and so will I. Not only because of the champagne but I know the French will love me and my books very much. Which reminds me, I have to get more pâté as soon as possible—makes my coat shine and makes me even more irresistible than usual. For who and what I don't know, but I am the best-looking cat in the world, and for me to know that is enough for me. Hmmm, maybe there is some Hollywood in me as John seems to think, and not just more money so he can drive around in a Bentley and make me wear a stupid chauffeur's cap. I have to watch him so close at times. That would be the last straw. Well, maybe not. I just don't want to wear the tuxedo that would go with it. Then again, if it would help his blood pressure, I would do it. He was thinking one day about getting a dog and that is quite a stretch. I guess if I am pressured I will wear a cat tuxedo and chauffeur's cap, but only once in a while. Anything to get his mind off a big dog that he wants, so I will be able to ride on the dog's back and give him and John directions. What the heck? It might be fun. For the immediate future, I will use what I know to help lower his pressure. If he "goes away" it will be a difficult job to get a replacement. I would miss all those jokes, and he likes the same things I like. Well, almost. Ahem.

Robert Frost Night

*I*t was a beautiful night. We were all at our favorite meeting place, the chimney, high above San Francisco, sitting on a roof, enjoying the sights. The spot where we were was one of the "power spots" of the world. It was a confluence of all of the various energies in the world, almost heaven. At least for a mind-reading cat such as I am. I am a twenty-pound silverpoint Siamese, simply, and completely beautiful, as they say. I live with my food friend, John, who is aware of my capabilities but, for the most part, treats me like anyone would treat a twenty-pound silverpoint Siamese cat—very carefully. Kidding completely aside, John is my best friend, and vice versa.

I was with more of my good friends, Seagull Joe, the big seagull who had the only air taxi service anywhere, come to think of it. My Uncle Al was there as well. We were all puffing gently on our newest invention, Castro's Cha Cha Cancer Killing Cigars. These special cigars came about as many great inventions do, accidentally. Upon "trading" for a boatload of Cuban cigars, some type of chemical was spilled on four thousand pounds of the cigars, and voila! We noticed something unusual in the puff, and so we took the cigars to a Stanford cancer scientific specialist. More voila! The interaction of the cigar and the chemical together gave the cigars a 100 percent cancer killing quality! Simple, when one smokes the cigar, they have no cancer worries anymore. I must add, it deals quite well with other bothersome worries, too, and you feel "All good!" No cancer, no worries! We can't make and puff them fast enough.

As we were sitting around the chimney, a big blackbird, quite startling scintillatingly, alighted on the edge of the chimney. Seagull Joe said, "I would like to introduce you to my good friend, Susie. She and her family live over on Pier 31. She has some very interesting information that I think you will want to hear."

I said, "Well, hello, Susie, my name is Casey."

"Hello!" she said. "Nice to be here. Listen to this! I just saw a giant submarine under the floor where I live."

"Wow!" I said.

"Wow! To you, too," she said. "It's a Russian sub, and they have nuclear warheads onboard. They are getting ready to blow up San Francisco, or anywhere else they can."

"Wow!" I said.

She said, "If you say *wow* one more time, I will leave!"

"So there," I said. "Is that better?"

"I heard you were a wisenheimer," she said, "so I will forgive your lack of professional courtesy."

"Thank you," I said. "Now, where did you see this giant sub?"

"Under the floor in my house, for the second time already, it is a big floor, a half mile long and wide. In WWII, it was used to build and launch all kinds of warships. At night the floor rolls back, and the sub pops up."

I almost said, "There is a joke in there somewhere," but I didn't. Instead, I said, "Wow!" Seagull Joe laughed, and so did Uncle Al. I thought I saw a hint of a smile on Susie's face, so I said, "Howzabout a cigar?"

She said, "You guys can't be serious about anything! Grrrrr!" She was getting her Russian up, or whatever her birth nationality was, and she was deadly serious. After a few puffs of the cigar, she settled down a bit. Uncle Al told her some silly cat jokes, and we all relaxed again. No need for fur to fly.

We were ready to take on the giant submarine beneath the floor of her house that was going to blow up "whatever it could." Wow, I did not say it out loud. It was a cat thought. 'Nuff to make a cat laugh! The cancer killing Cuban Cha Cha Cigar did what it does best, it intensified and solidified her thoughts so as to make what she said completely understandable to all the rest of us. Susie told us that at night, big eighteen-wheeler semis came in, loaded, and offloaded material. It was a synchronized maneuver, and only took one half hour. I made a personal visit as well to the sub, and verified all she had said. (Cats can go anywhere.) A man named Igor had his gnarled hand on a red button, really, ready at any moment to flip the switch, setting off nuclear destruction to all. Meanwhile, trucks came and went. The floor rolled up before morning and no one was the wiser except for us cats. A plan was made.

One of the trucks servicing the sub was a water truck. It held four thousand gallons of water and was offloaded every day. We "compromised" the water truck, and filled it to the brim with the best Russian vodka on the planet, 179 proof, tasted like water, even better, slid down so smooth. Four thousand gallons of 179-proof vodka was pumped down into the sub, their total "water" supply for one day. Ten minutes after pumping all the "water" aboard, two hundred drunken, naked men were walking off the sub with military drunken precision. They headed straight for the Transamerica Skyscraper. They were totaled, and totally happy. Each one had a gallon flask and took solid sips as they walked naked down Columbus Street to the skyscraper. Everyone on Columbus Street thought it was a parade. It had to be. Two hundred naked men, completely wasted and holding on to the buzz with a giant flask of 179-proof vodka. They walked into the skyscraper and went directly to the top floor, passed out, and were arrested forever. Too much, even for San Francisco! "Someone" alerted the authorities to the happenings at Pier 31, and all was taken care of automatically and silenced. Susie thanked us and said, "Now, all my kids can get some sleep!"

I said, "Wow!"

A New World Order

Somehow, I had come upon the randomness of the universe, and it decided to leave me with every iota of knowledge, information on you name it, that was, is, and will ever be. (Sounds like bee talk, wazz, wiz, and zzzzzzz.) I had as my go-between, or go wherever I needed him to, a man who had just won one billion dollars. Lucky? You think? We had it all, seemed to be anyhow, money and moxie. (I must have picked up that word from a Damon Runyon book that I had stored in my mind along with quantum physics.) All we had to do was follow what was in my mind with the situations that were dealt us and handle them properly. We had it made. Now, I had to make sure John didn't blow the billion and leave me trying to find someone else who could drive a car and take me around.

My abilities to read minds, commute telepathically, and use "appropriate mental persuasion" were a great help. I could also do much more, and every day more information was coming to me. Somehow, I was able to process it all with no worry or fuss. Sometimes I downloaded a bit to John to see how he would handle it. (He had a lot of storage space.) He understood, gave me a wink like a Chinese cat, got a beer, sat down, and watched the football game. Mostly, we went out. He would put me in my backpack and off we went. Since he now had some extra cash, he could go where he wanted, and eat and drink what he wanted. I, too, did what I wanted. I enjoyed myself in the backpack as people would come up and say, "Oh, you've got a cat in your backpack." John would say, "Yes, he is a care cat, very special. He carries what I need with him in his orange care cat jacket." The people would then buy us whatever we wanted. Made me think maybe all he really needs is me.

With my mind-reading abilities I could tell at all times what people were thinking. I soon learned it was mostly chatter of some sort. One mind was quite different. It was a woman's. She sat down next to us as this was the only chair available in the restaurant and said, "Hello." John replied in kind. Since he was now stinko rich, but he told no one, he asked if she would like a drink. She said, "No thanks, buy my own." The plot thickened. I peeked into John's mind, and he was laughing. *All this dough and now I can't even buy a woman a drink, when before... Oh, what the heck?* (Wasn't heck, but you get the idea.) In a short while, they were talking about what people talk about. Where are you from, what do you do, and blah blah. John said he was a cat carrier. New test program for people with conditions who had to be monitored all the time. She was interested and asked if she could touch me. Hmmmm? They usually say pet me. John said, "Love to let you but can't. Casey here has to have as little human contact as possible in order to keep his cat care persona as one with me."

She said, "Excellent! I should have known, but he is so beautiful."

I smiled and for a millisecond looked into her mind. Pretty is as pretty does, and although pretty on the outside, she was quite different on the inside. I read the evil intentions of her mind. The conversation continued, as did the libations, and then it was time to go. They smiled, said thanks, and off we went. I gave John a few quick cat-bats and told him mentally what she wanted. We immediately got in a cab and headed home. She wanted to kidnap John. "Kidnap the kidder?" John said. I was in no mood for jokes. Cats are very serious, and I was so happy with John's jokes because he can make a cat laugh, but this was not a laughing matter. I communicated to him the seriousness of the situation and what must be done. I thought I heard John growl; maybe he is not so jocular after all. (But he still is very funny.)

As it happens, John is of Irish and Germanic descent. Tall, well built, well spoken, intelligent, excellent facial structure, a look and a bearing that makes all take a second look or sometimes three. (Hope he doesn't read this.) Ahem! At this time on the planet, a new world order was taking place. The order needed a leader who could look, talk, walk, be, and say what they wanted him to be. They needed to get that person (it was John!), put him in place, and then begin their conquest of the world. They were the Nazis. Hitler's own flesh had come to rise, and they needed, well, a new Hitler. (I started to laugh almost uncontrollably, real bad manners for a cat, and then I realized John could very well be one of Hitler's offspring. Hitler's sperm had been kept and used scientifically for many years.) After searching everywhere, they had found what they wanted, and just when I was thinking about having John get a Mercedes.

Our first order of business was to disappear. Since John carries about $100K with him in the trunk of his car, that was no problem. We could go anywhere and hide out for a long time. But phooey, that was not going to happen. We were going to put those nutty Nazis out of business. Their headquarters was in Idaho, where lots of land and lots of politicians could be bought off. They ran and/or owned about half the state. I immediately got in contact with my paws-on-the-ground friends and my eyes-in-the-skies friends as well. We found out exactly where they lived, and where all the backbone and firepower of the Nazis was congregated. We also knew about all of the feeder veins that helped to keep the creeps up and running. A plan was formulated to begin at a precise time in every one of their places of creepiness. At that exact time, the paws and fur on the ground and the feathers and eyes in the skies would execute a plan that would, well, execute the Nazis out of business. A chemical had been invented by the Nazis themselves. When put in your drinking water, it starts a chain reaction in the cells that feed upon each other. It only takes about a week to kill one slowly, and that's all you need to know for now. (Don't want to let the cat entirely out of the bag.) The chemical was dispersed, and immediately massive convulsive behavior by a good deal of people in Idaho began. When the chemical acted on a person's cells, absolutely no sign of a body remained when the chemical work was completed. Idaho lost a lot of nuts rapidly and invisibly.

Not much was made of it because the people who were gone were the ones who were causing all the problems. Clean sweep... I never thought John was right for the job anyhow. He hates wearing suits, won't wave, and he doesn't walk like he has cobs in his pants. Ahem!

Rolex Man

*E*xcuuuse me! My name is Casey, and I can't help it if I weigh *about* twenty pounds! It runs in the family. (Isn't that a dandy excuse for everything?) I am a Siamese silverpoint with big blue eyes. (Please hold the jokes on my family moniker bloodline until I am finished here.) My color is a creamy gray, and I can stretch out to about three feet. I am a big kitty. I am also very strong and fast, and the pièce de résistance is that I can read minds. Enough of that for now! I live with my good buddy, John, who is a human. (I had to clarify that since so many animals have human names.) We get along famously and go everywhere together. Whether we get out of the train, car, plane, or boat, I ride along with him in a backpack. Whatta deal! When people see us coming, they are agog if I stick my head and paws out of the backpack. Love that backpack! I can sleep or stand up inside, and take a look around to make sure John is not getting into trouble. Trouble happens often with John's adventures.

We went into one of John's favorite restaurants here in the great city of San Francisco. (Hold it a second… "I Left My Heart in San Francisco," Antonio Benedetti. Feel so much better when I hum that song as I write about San Francisco.) Let's see…where was I? Oh, yeah. While at the restaurant, I stood up and looked around with my paws on John's shoulders. A very nice-looking lady came over to where we were standing and said, "Oh my, what a beautiful creature!" I said nothing, but looked at her with my very large Siamese blue cat eyes. I think they were tinted green that day. (It was almost

St. Paddy's Day.) She went on. "Oh, so beautiful and soft, and blah, blah, blah…"

John said, "Why, thank you. People rarely say that about me anymore. Why, I remember the time…"

"Oh no," she said, "not you—that beautiful cat in the backpack."

Laughter went all around, and John said, "Well, it's good to hear those words directed towards me anyway. I'll accept some of the compliment just to make me feel good—cheap thrills."

The conversation continued, and she kept looking at me and sipping on something. She finally said, "May I touch the cute kitty?" (Harrumph, I am not a kitty! Tigers are my close ancestors, and believe me, they come out of the chute ready to go. Me, too! But I must play the role people expect of me.)

"Sure," John said. "He's friendly most of the time."

She reached up and patted me lightly on the back and said, "Oh, my goodness, his fur is the most luxurious I have ever felt, and those eyes! I wonder if he would like some caviar—Russian caviar, of course, the very best!" I meowed with purrfect timing, and out came the caviar, and me out of the backpack, purring and walking close to the lady's legs, rubbing up against them. (Schmoozing always helps with these sorts of things.)

John said, "It's going to take a lot of caviar to fill Casey up, just kidding. He is always a gentleman, and he does have only one bad habit."

The lady said, "Pray tell." (The conversation was getting kind of thick, but I was still doing my standard cat act.) "What might that be?"

John replied, "If you ever play cards with him, he will insist on winning. Even if you win, he won't pay up, and he can cause quite a fuss. When you called him a kitty, I was glad he didn't hear you. As you can see, he is a tiger in a cat's body." (Boy, did I love John then! I must remember to make sure he stays with this brand of booze wherever we go.) She was in complete awe, as was I while I was eating a dish of caviar. Meow!

After eating, I went into the backpack while their conversation continued... *Humans*, I thought. I hung my tail out of the backpack a bit, so as to keep her attention on me. John needed help. Funny, he can talk to me, but he can't talk to women very well at all. Makes me laugh! I pulled my cat tail in and was having a wonderful caviar cat dream nap when the hair on my back stood straight up. Uh oh! What did John do now?!

Nope, it wasn't John at all. It was a loud crazy man yelling and waving a handgun around, telling everybody to just shut up and get down on the floor! He fired a gunshot into the ceiling. (I knew because I had jumped out of the backpack by then and was under a chair discreetly watching these events take place.) The gunman said, "Take out everything from your pockets, take off all your valuables, and place them in a bucket!" As he walked by, he pumped two more shots into the huge mirror behind the bar, which made a really huge cracking sound as the glass shattered everywhere, startling the customers. Some were crying, moaning, and even yelping. They were taking off their valuables and getting out their money, pronto! Let's face it, they were scared, big time. Lying face down in a fashionable San Francisco restaurant with gunshots and crashing glass will get your attention and complicity pretty fast. Besides, the bar room floor wasn't the best place to have your nose to the ground. The man continued to yell, "Stay still! Do what I say!" They did, but not me. John and I were "talking" to each other. We were ready to go for it. Too bad for John, in that he was lying right next to that beautiful, gorgeous lady, but it was on a stinky bar room floor. Not exactly how he wanted to be next to her given the choice. So what, if it hadn't been for me, she would have been talking to the guy with the 200K gold Rolex.

Our plan to get the crook was simple, as most good plans are. I would walk up behind him, and then do what cats have been doing for eons—walk between his legs and trip him good. I would give him a little extra by taking a chunk out of his femoral artery. Ouch, but very effective! Besides, I needed the exercise.

It all happened in a flash with total communication between me and John. As soon as I tripped the gunman and bit the phooey out of him, John literally jumped on the guy's back while he was down. John was quick and strong. He told me he had played for the Los Angeles Rams, and I gave it one "Meow!" Now, I will sing to him the Tony Bennett song, "I Love You So Much!" John was a blur of strength and quickness. (Exactly like my tiger ancestors, I thought to myself. Hmmm, you don't suppose? Naw, couldn't be.) In about two seconds, the guy was totally squished, his gun taken away, and he was knocked unconscious. Then John let out a helluva growl! I jumped up on the bar, so as to make everyone think it was me. It was totally all right for him to knock the guy silly, and break an arm and a leg, but to let them even think for a millisecond that he was transformed into some kind of tiger cat would never do. They would never let him have a drink in that bar again. Luckily, most of the people had their faces in their drinks and were still gasping from being so familiar with the stinky floor. Anything John had done was barely noticed by anyone except me. The rest could easily be explained away—the dim lighting, the booze, the fear and screaming while confusion reigned. I jumped into the backpack while the owner of the bar and restaurant yelled out, "Drinks on the house! Oh yes, and get that cat some more caviar!" I was declared the hero of the day. It was "decided" the robber had faltered awkwardly when he tripped and had fallen on a steak knife, and my growling from on top of the bar had totally confused him as well. It all fit together nicely. John got a free tall glass of his vodka tonic drink, and the gorgeous lady we had just met went over to schmooze with the fancy Rolex watch guy who worked at the Bank of Switzerland. She had a sense that she saw what John did out of the corner of her eye. *Who needs that around the house?* she thought. *I'm going for the gold!* "But, hmmmm," I heard her say, "I did kind of like that growl!"

San Francisco Under Siege

*I*t was our usual night with Uncle Al and I, except his seagull taxi, Seagull Joe, decided to stay after he dropped Al off at our meeting place at the chimney. We were high above the city of San Francisco, where great plans, ideas, and whatever needs to be done anywhere can be discussed, and action decided upon or not. Seagull Joe said, "Why don't you give that cigar a rest before we all choke?"

Al said, "This is one of the best things in the world one can do for oneself, or don't you keep up with the Castro cigar invention that has effectively cured cancer throughout the world?"

"Whatever," Joe said disdainfully, "just as long as you pay your taxi fare, I won't complain. I am also crazy about those new dumpsters in the city you find for me—that helps me out with feeding my family."

Al continued to puff, and we were soon enveloped in blue-gray clouds of smoke along with the mysterious scent that is believed to be the cancer-curing agent.

But I was very concerned about what I had found out recently. There was a return of about thirty-five hippies who were a long way from being flower children, and they had caused death and delirium in the city by selling poisoned, altered drugs that were killing people. They were planning on returning to the city and killing all within its borders by chemical spray warfare. They had just returned from prison, and my, how they were bitter. They wanted retribution for their years spent in that doggone terrible place. I presented the problem to Joe and Al, and Al puffed even harder. Seagull Joe was giving me the bird eye. I told them what I wanted to do, and that it would involve as many seagulls as Joe could get together. Al and I would coordinate the seagulls when it all started, and all they had to do was what seagulls do best. Bombs away, so to speak! For the next ten days, all the seagulls that Joe could get together from everywhere would have free oats in an abandoned boxcar in the railroad yard. I would fill them up, give them lots of energy, and get them prepared for big bombing raids that would be necessary to stop the hippies and their dastardly scheme. Our plan was to fly, flatulate, and then bombs away.

At that very second, in a fully equipped high-tech Greyhound bus, the evil plan was being readied to kill all the people in San Francisco and its environs. The plan was simple and direct. Drive the bus into the exact center of center, and spray the poison all over. All would be dead who smelled the gas in minutes. Two million dead was the projected result. I knew their plan as my cat messengers throughout the peninsula had reported in and told me the exact time and date when the bus would come out of its underground hideout and begin its trip of death. All we had to do was to wait for the bus to come out, and alert Seagull Joe and his boys, er, birds, and we would begin.

Two days later, as we knew they would, the bus emerged, and so did Seagull Joe and all his crew. Approximately one hundred thousand seagulls, plumb full of oats and the mixture in a seagull's body that all those oats bring about, began making bombing raids on the bus. Again and again from fifty feet away from the ground in San

Francisco, the busy birds dropped pile after pile on the bus as it rumbled down the road. The further it got, the slower it rumbled until it was crossing the Golden Gate Bridge and was blinded by the greatest bird bombing the world has ever known. It became too much for the driver to see about halfway across the bridge, and it zigged and zagged, and hopped the bridge railing in doing so. Three hundred feet below, it smashed into the 52-degree Pacific Ocean outgoing tide and began to sink. Slowly but surely, it began its way to the bottom when for the last time the hippie decided to "light one up." As he did, the flame from the match ignited the tremendous amount of methane gas dumped on it by the bird bombers, and kaboom went the bus of destruction! Wow! That was some huge chemical explosion! As they say in Texas, "Chew, it leaves your hands free." Now, they also say, "Don't flatulate and fire!" Meow!

Full Moon

erfect moon out tonight. People usually associate full moons with cats, so since cats don't care, why not take a look at the moon? So many songs have been written about the moon. I hear them being played all the time on the radio. Beautiful songs, so romantic; it fits perfectly with me. I'm not romantic for a cat, but people look at me and say, "Oh, what a pretty kitty!" and such. Okay, just don't sneeze on me, and please mix in some mouthwash with that terrible breath people have. Fortunately, all my senses are so highly developed that I can stay away from unpleasant things and circumstances, almost always. Only time things go a bit awry is when John takes me somewhere, and I have to go along with the scene. What the heck, I am a care cat, aren't I? Some perfume I will not tolerate at all. I told John, "No perfume from those ladies with those frumpy dresses and faces to match who are chewing their gums and patting their hair constantly." Young women have come up with some type of a stink that they rub on themselves, and it is horrible as well. (Uncle Al loves all smells, but we won't go there, now or ever. One of his favorite things is to get in an elevator when people are going to work and take in a few strong whiffs. Knock 'em out, Al. Oops, I said I wouldn't go there, but couldn't resist. But Al is different. People say cats have nine lives, and they are wrong. Al will never die.)

The moon is still out, and it is eight in the morn. I love it. Maybe we cats do have something to do with the moon. More than the radio station Coast to Coast for sure. What a bunch of nuts! All conjecture and it gets John in a strange mood. Then I have to earn my cat care moniker. I brush my tail over his forehead, one small meaningful meow, and that usually takes care of him. I only had to cat-bat him a few times. He was sleeping fitfully, and the dream was about alligators. I batted him, and we got up and went for a drive. He started to sing along with some song on the radio, and I threw in a few meows as well. John started laughing, and like I always say, who is taking care of whom?

We took a drive to the beach, and I hopped right out and checked out the immediate area. I will always have my cat instincts, and they include making sure wherever you are is completely safe. (Kind of like being a general in the marines, but I will not fight, I avoid it. Cat intelligence is so far advanced beyond anything anybody knows. We couldn't care less. When you are the most beautiful girl at the prom dance, why worry?)

The area was safe. I checked on John, and he was checking on me and had a smile on his face. He was thinking about the show where a cat drove an alligator back into the water after the gator hissed at the cat. They cat-batted him four times, and the stupid gator crawled back to his filthy lair. John was hoping a fish would show up so I could bat it around. He likes action. He likes me to be in on the action while he watches and has a laugh or two. I might show my stuff with a couple of crabs and chase some beach birds around, but that is about all. If there are people around and he wants to meet them, I will go over and give it a look. I better keep a closer check on that guy. He wanted to take me to Hollywood so I could get a part and he would take the money. Now he wants me to be some kind of a beach cat. I do it naturally. If it wasn't natural, I wouldn't do it. Maybe, but I think he has me addicted to wiping my paws clean three or four times a day. He heard on the radio that cats walk in their "stuff" and then spread it around wherever they walk. That woke him up. Next thing I know, he is cleaning my paws with a towel and peroxide quite a bit. I don't mind it, but I am rather insulted that he thinks I walk in my "stuff." Maybe Uncle Al does, but not me. I am extremely clean and I will make a statement that should be noticeable everywhere, all the time. Some cats use the human facilities. Harrumph! I even flush! No cause of concern to me at all. The less humans know about cats the better. As long as they continue to smear their bodies with all kinds of stinky stuff and eat like alligators, they will never progress. At least John doesn't do that. He needs work, but in the meantime, he does and says things that are enough to make a cat laugh.

The shadow of the moon is still in the sky, and it will be another beautiful moonlit night. John woke up at three in the morn and thought it was seven. He likes to get up early and try to catch me sleeping, but it will never happen. Like some people put chips in their animals, I have put a "chip" in John, kind of. It is actually a mental alert that I am tuned into constantly. I guess it is like mothers have with their children, and please don't go there. I am not a mother. But he needs constant watching, so at the very least all my training will not be in vain, and I may have to get "another" one. I could always be like some cats and go all around the world and take on different companions constantly, but that is not for me. Maybe he does have me addicted to wiping my paws with peroxide. So what? He changes my water every day, almost. He clips my nails when they need it. I could do it, but yanking on them or crawling around on roofs looking for chimneys or pawing on the sidewalk to trim my nails is not what I would give style points for. This is about as complicated as it gets with rules on cat care.

Meanwhile, the full moon will be out for sixteen hours tonight, and I will be on extra alert to see what happens. "Awctually" I know what will happen, and where, and I will just make sure I am not near those places. Besides, the movie *North by Northwest* is on tonight, and I want to watch it. If John goes to sleep early, it is okay. I will have the couch all to myself that way. I love Hitchcock movies, and did you know he lived near Santa Cruz, California? I have been there a few times, and the woods are full of animals. Big ones looking for a meal, and I don't want style points for that kind of action either. I see where I seem to be concerned about style points. I am. They keep me alive or, at the very least, keep me from having to run the mile in under three minutes or swim in cold water. Or, having John smile at me when I show up soaking wet and saying to me, "You're going to end up in Hollywood one way or another." Hummph! Whatever that means. Meow!

Come Fly With Me, but Be Careful

The title of this chapter, "Come Fly With Me," is a fantastic song with great lyrics and music. The flying capital of the world is Area 51, but as the comment on the title of the chapter says, be careful. Not long ago in Area 51 a very strange occurrence happened. A truck driver pushing an eighteen-wheeler straight out of Boeing from Seattle to the infamous area saw a very weird thing. Wherever he looked, it was upside down. He gathered himself, pulled off to the side of the road, and called "home," a number that was only to be used in the utmost crucial circumstances of his profession. He worked for the most secretive military organization in the world. When their number was reached it was, well, as we cats would say, *let's get out of here*. He explained as well as he could that everything was upside down, and it was the most impossible circumstance he had ever been in. He wanted to be told what to do. There was no answer.

Three days later reports began to come in throughout the world about the strange event that took place just outside of Los Alamos, New Mexico. It was completely indescribable, except that's what it was. I had no choice but to call my—don't tell anyone—alien compatriots. They told me what had happened. Area 51 had been experimenting with various weapons that would not injure humans, but would cause great confusion, and if used on an enemy, would make them helpless. The aliens called this the upside-down bomb. It would, when launched, turn everything upside down that was hit by its blast. It would stay that way for about two days, which would give the attackers time enough to get control and simply win the fight. All of that sounds great if you are the one who has the weapon. Obviously something went awry since you tested your own weapons on your own people. You think?

John was speaking about it, I took note, and that night we boys gathered together around the chimney that has helped us with so many great ideas and actions thereof. It is a chimney high above the city of San Francisco that gives one 360 degrees visibly and mentally. Truly, one of the greatest spots on the face of the earth, where all the powers that be can be gathered and used for good. (Cats only do good anyhow, except for Uncle Al, and all he does once in a while is keep his paw on the scale when he sells catnip.) I brought up the upside-down weapon, and of course, all had heard of it. Now we talked about what had happened and how to control it.

An upside-down bomb does what it is named. It doesn't bother cats because we have a built-in gyroscope that keeps us perfectly aligned no matter what. Other living things are not so lucky. If you have a lot of change in your pants, you will lose it immediately, your purse will empty out completely, your valise full of valuable papers will go floating away, money trucks will have all the money going everywhere, and you can imagine the moral implications as well with women upside down with their dresses above their heads. Need I meow more?

Big trouble, and we had to solve it in the blink of an eye. A plan was made, and off we went. Seagull Joe took the lead, and two of his best flyers were with him. Uncle Al and I got on the birds, and we went to Los Alamos. It was easy to get in and in no time, we were in the building which held all the secrets of the upside-down bomb. Now, to find out who set it off and why. I used my mind-reading abilities and immediately came upon a professor of the upside-down bomb locked in a closet. We freed him. I put him under cat sedation, and he told us what happened. A group calling itself the Big Boys had tunneled from below and captured him and the weapon. They forced him to tell them how to use it and in their excitement forgot about him in the lab. They had the weapon, and they were going to use it on New York City. (Several comments were made by the birds, such as "That place is already upside down, so what's the big deal," and so on. I mentally turned one's mind upside down for a few seconds while he was flying, and he understood immediately. He had defecated on himself. Now he knew the danger.)

We knew where they were going because they did not cover up their tunnel, so we just followed the tunnel. About five miles south of Phoenix, we could hear them moving about and going to NYC as fast as they could. We cheated. The professor had given us a hand-held upside-down bomb, and we turned it on them. In less than a minute, they were helpless. The Big Boys had become big boogers. Area 51 folks came along and cleaned up the mess, and we flew off with Seagull Joe and his two able companions. Upon coming back to our office, The Chimney, we were very pleased with ourselves. At that very second, a Big Boy appeared on the corner of the roof, and in no time, Uncle Al turned him upside down with the handheld device he had "borrowed" from Area 51. Big Boy lost all his money and his ID. We threw him off the roof, where he landed in a moat and was arrested by a feminist policewoman and taken away. May I say, the upside-down bomb can't hold a candle to a San Francisco feminist policewoman. All along the best weapon was right where we lived. Just be sure you don't go for a midnight swim naked, with tattoos of Rush Limbaugh on your bum, and you should be safe.

Mystery and Spies

*I*n the mysterious world of Never Never, John was trapped. My dreams had gotten out of control, as if one can control a dream anyhow. I could not get out of this dream, and I did not know if I was awake or asleep. Seemed all right sometimes, but then again, I would find myself in London not knowing how I got there and standing on top of Big Ben waving at people. Not right. They, the all-powerful they, might catch me. That would be twice as bad, getting caught when you are already caught, so you think. While I was in this dream of reality or make-believe, I could almost do whatever I wanted, all legal, of course. While I was in London, for example, I stayed at the Savoy, ate at their lounge, compliments of management, and had some suits fitted on Saville Row. Boy, I looked like a poor man's James Bond. I'll take it. I mean as Sean Connery now, and except for Roger Moore, those other guys were so fake, I thought.

It just so happened there was a Bond movie being made. I walked right on the set and got the James Bond role immediately. I was told what to do, and directed to go to the set, and off we went. We—that would be me and my buddy Casey, a cat (huh?)—and two women from Brazil who couldn't keep their eyes or emotions off me for a second. Whew! But I was up to the part, and I treated them in a manly way as the script directions were for my character to do.

We were chasing the most villainous person ever conceived. He would do anything to get more women, and he also wanted to steal the only mind-reading cat in the world. Aha, that's why I have the cat! The women are just for fun and distraction, but Casey, my cat, is the real McCoy. Oh, boy! Somehow, you know how dreams are, we all ended up on the same gigantic ocean liner, three times as big as the biggest one ever, almost a half mile long and nearly as wide. The villain, his name was Earl—kind of a weak name for the top villain, but that's what drove him on. He hated his name, Earl, because he said it sounded so stupid. He wanted to control everything to make people love him and all that, but he still didn't have the mind-reading cat. He also knew the cat was with two "foxes," an old Steve Martin reference to good-looking women, and I was in charge of the trio. We had to catch him. He had to have the cat and the foxes.

As the great ocean liner crossed the seas of the world, Earl commanded his troops to do his evil bidding. He was going to rule the world of crime. He had the usual mad scientist doctor whose specialty was bringing back people from the grave and giving them life. They were going to bring back Churchill and Hitler, and then start WWII all over. Whatta script!

But strangely, as I was seeing and doing all these things, I was unable to differentiate between what was and was not real. Was I really the new James Bond? Were these women and this mind-reading cat really under my control? Was this a real ship? Was this actually not a script, but the real deal? I was convinced that this was the real world. Maybe a dream world, but the consequences would be the same. I had to capture Earl, stupid name and all, and stop another WWII.

We were firmly ensconced in a room right next to the main kitchen. A sliding panel in the wall enabled us to go in and out and get whatever we wanted. We were also able to see what dishes they were preparing and for whom. The kitchen was as big as a basketball court. They had every kind of food in the world. Believe it! Helicopters brought in daily whatever the passengers dreamed up. As for us, we ate the leftovers, so as not to let anyone know we were there. Casey, my cat, ate most of it. Sally and Sophie just walked around the room, looked at me, and brought me cigars and such.

We knew if we could figure out what Earl was eating, all we had to do was put a little "snuff" in his food and that would be that. We also installed a peephole in the ceiling so we could see the dishes that were being prepared. Fantastic! We almost forgot why we were there. Every kind of dish from all around the world was prepared instantly by the best chefs ever. You name it, they could cook it. Most of the food was funky to me. One taco after another, and somebody had ordered a whole hog. Aha! The game was afoot. Earl was eating hog day and night. All we had to do was find out where the hog was sent, and bingo, no more Earl and his mad plans.

My cat, Casey, had a great plan. All we had to do was find a rabbi who would bless the hog, and the kosher food would kill Earl and his mad scientist instantly. Easy to say, but not to do. Aha! We did find a rabbi. I could not believe it. It was Mel Brooks. Oy vey! I told him wat whas the plot, scheamatics, the whole schmere, and he immediately blessed all the hogs on the ship, and in Nebraska, because that's where most hogs lived. Sure enough, shortly after, we saw via the ceiling camera that there was a hog being prepared and delivered. Ten minutes later, a "Get the hell out of the way!" siren was blasting. The word was that two people were very sick and had to be taken to Vienna. Oy vey again! You guessed it. Earl and his buddy were shipped out, and if not dead, looked like the people they were trying to bring to life. It was a great moment and Mel and I yucked it up. Sally, Sophie, and Casey went to sleep after hearing more Jewish jokes than you can believe. But I had to stay awake and play the part of James Bond. I told Mel if I heard one more bad joke, I was going to throw him overboard. Mel said, "Really? This ship is so damn big I can't even see the ocean. It would be a pleasure." Well, we all started to laugh, and Casey brought out the cards and cigars. We had beaten the devil once more. A dead kosher hog had saved the world. Oy vey!

Put Silver Wings on My Son's Chest

I guess you may have heard the Green Beret song whose title is at the head of this chapter. Uncle Al had never heard it before, and when he did, because he has some kind of a "high tech" center where he keeps a radio, TV, and you can only guess what else, he got hold of me immediately. He was meowing and purring and whirling his tail, batting the air like a boxer while standing on his hind feet and walking around our favorite chimney, which was high above the city of San Francisco on a high and windy night. It was a beautiful night, about 54 degrees, wind coming in out of the south/southwest at about eight miles an hour with unlimited visibility. At that very moment, we were looking toward Alcatraz Island and watching the *Ronald Reagan* aircraft carrier swiftly making its way past Alcatraz, going under the Golden Gate Bridge and heading out for only what the captain and secretary of defense have privy to secretly. I felt fantastic and content, and I told you how Al felt. Then Al pulled out a cigar and took a few puffs. I knew then something dynamic and historic was about to take place. As the puffs of smoke curled around Al's head, my head, the chimney, and almost the entire roof—thank goodness for the breeze—he began to describe to me what he would like to do. That by doing what he was telling me would make America once and for all time the absolute leader, backed with sheer delight by all the people on the planet. (Animals as well, but animals are most always happy, especially cats, so now Al figured it was only right to give people some hope.)

This was Al's plan! Al was going to fly a fighter F-14 off the *Ronald Reagan* aircraft carrier and do what was necessary to make sure there would be peace throughout the entire world for once and for all. (Al's favorite saying recently, "For once and for all." He just loved it.) He invited me to come along, actually told me he needed me, since he did not know much about celestial navigation, reading maps in general, how to put gas in a jet, when the carrier would be in port, and how much food we would need for the trip. Other than that, he had figured out everything else down to a cat's whisker, and that if I supplied him with the info (Al was now dropping down into Air Force lingo), we would be a "go" as soon as possible. Okay! As it turned out the carrier was due back in port in two days. I would have all the info he needed, and we would take off and convince the world that America is what we all need for true happiness and comfort. It would put so many smiles on people's faces that the glare on a sunny day would mean millions more sunglasses sales, and I had to slow him down. Al is positively mercurial, runs on highest octane whatever, but sometimes he needs to be pointed in the right direction. I guess it's what some people call creativity or artistic ability, but I call it too much of something in those Havana cigars. Just maybe. Ahem!

Two nights later we were on the carrier, seated in the cockpit with our specially made oxygen masks and clothing and ten cans of cat food. Al said when we stopped to get "gassed up", we could always get whatever we want, more cigars even. Al pushed some buttons on the dash, and the floor began to move. Three men with flashlights and helmets showed us the way to the carrier floor, lowered the wings, and backed the F-14 up against the blasting wall. We were all set. Two minutes later, we got the signal with men waving us to take off. Al hit the throttle, and in no time, we were six miles above San Francisco and our favorite chimney. Exhilarating! To make sure everything was running smoothly, we didn't want to go back and get another one, Al popped a few barrel rolls and some hemmys, and now, New York, here we come!

Since New York is actually the capital of the world, Al thought it would be necessary to get its attention and its support before we visited the rest of the world. Traveling at 1,000 mph gets one to anywhere in one helluva hurry, but this was not good enough for Al. The plane we had was the top plane the Air Force had, with capabilities to go up to 2,000 mph. Now we were cookin'! We radioed ahead and told New York we were going to visit them to prove to them everything was fine. We were going to show them exactly what this plane could do, in effect what America could do. We would then go all over the world and visit the various capitals and anywhere else that needed convincing, and show them what we could do.

We were in New York in three hours, which gave us plenty of time to have a bite to eat, take a few puffs (there weren't any "no smoking" signs). Al even snuck in some Russian life-giving water because he was sure that was a great selling point. I'm glad he didn't check into some of the other life-giving water that other countries have, or we might have had to leave off a wheel or two.

Upon reaching New York, we did exactly what we told them we would do, and put on a show. Because we also had a cloaking shield that no radar or the human eye could see through, it was like flying a Piper Cub on a Sunday afternoon over the church parade. We went up and down 5th Avenue a couple of times, zipped in and out of Yankee Stadium (during a game, no less), and we went through Harlem and dropped some nasty gas that made it easy for the troops to arrest every gangbanger and law breaker that ever was or would be. Not just in Harlem, but in that entire town, and it needed it. We also dropped a case of 7-Up on the mayor's house. (The next day he was voted out of office, and they voted us in, but we passed it on to Yogi Berra and Jimmy Walker, in absentia. We were so proud!) Five minutes later, after covering every square inch of New York, we had totally convinced the capital of the world that they were in the best hands in the world, and to exude their enthusiasm forever and to everyone. We buzzed Wall Street twice and cranked off a sound barrier blast right in the heart (the heel).

The next day gas was at 25 cents a gallon and we were told it would be that way forever. The insurance mess was cleared up. We also dropped more nasty gas on all the people where they live, and places where they run around in black sheets that completely obscure their bodies and whatever bombs they are carrying underneath. It was suddenly stated in the *NY Times* that boatloads of people in black sheets were headed out to sea, and by dusk, there was not "hide nor hair" of them, or the absolutely lousy things they made.

The people who make up the backbone of New York City, bless those wonderful, humorous, life-loving human beings who said it best about the sheet people. NOTHING! All their possessions were melted down. Cape Canaveral was consulted, and rockets fired off straight into the sun. (There might be a few more weeks of heat when it is all said and done.) Then again, all that weird junk might blow up the sun, but it was a well-thought-out, calculated risk. On the way out, we dropped thousands of flowers on our Lady of Liberty. Despite our great speed and noise of the rocket at six miles up in the air, we could hear a great roar coming up to greet us and wish us well on our mission of peace. (I think I saw the new mayor, Yogi Berra, singing "God Bless America" from the Empire State Building and taking a puff on one of Uncle Al's cigars. Oops, dropped it, but he recovered in time, caught it, and made a snap throw to the crowds below.)

It took us two more days to travel throughout the world and promote our message in about one hundred cities. Smashing success! Before we got to Chicago, they had heard of what we did, were doing, and everyone in the town was singing "Chicago, Chicago"! A tear almost came down my whisker, but Al had lit up another cigar and was starting to doze, so I had to take over for a while. It was success upon success, and the world was completely united. Some say the success was mainly due to America's great technology, which was able to broadcast to the world instantaneously the exuberant and necessary actions that took place to bring the world together at once. Some say it was Yogi Berra singing atop the Empire State Building, but Al and I really know because cats love everybody. Simple cats, but we are greatly misunderstood. To be brutally truthful, in a land very unfriendly to all and to themselves, and it pains me greatly to say this, they've been eating us and our children for thousands of years. When this horrid country, or however people want to describe that conglomeration of what makes up the lowest kind of life form on this planet, became aware of what was happening, they attempted to take drastic measures. They were going to destroy the entire world.

All was in place. Every cat in the world knew about it. What to do? Cats are also heroic, completely unselfish, intelligent, and wear exquisite mink coats everywhere, all the time. These beautiful cats knew what to do. At the command center of this horrid group of people was where the weapons of mass destruction were kept. As these horrid people prepared to blast the entire world to poisonous smithereens, the cats sacrificed many of their own so the world could continue. Every cat at once in that awful country meowed for ten straight hours as loudly and creatively as they could. Total confusion, much like that of Babylon's Tower of Babel took place, but one of those most horrid humans of all was able to make it to the command center to set off the explosion. The center was being guarded by us, the guys in the mink coats. We had locked the lid, so the bomb imploded back upon them and rid the world of those creeps once and for all.

So, smile when you see a kitty or hear a meow. They love you completely. It's just tough being so wonderful, and they hope you understand.

The World of Women Completely Explained

I really don't have much to do with the opposite sex—women, fe-males, female cats, or even female humans. One peek in their minds and it is very confusing. No progress is being made or even attempted there. I understand that, but I like production. Take Uncle Al, please! (In memory of Henny Youngman, one of the best!) He is continually doing something or planning something. Of late, his seagull service, where he rides the big birds free anywhere at any time, is inventive, highly energized, not to worry about planning and protection. Uncle Al is always on some kind of a job or precipice of another. Doing, going, moving, laughing, meowing, Uncle Al is the best. I like that. To have none of the above is like a hamburger with all bun. Maybe that best describes the female for me. All bun, but then what? Bun and butt (punning aside, almost) not for me. I realize they are necessary for civilization. Wait, stop the presses. Do I hear and read where they may not be necessary? What with cloning and such? Now, I don't want to exclude females a bit. It's just that they are not much fun for me. No big deal. I just want action, positive, pro-gressive, invigorating, humorous, brilliant, spontaneous, effervescent action. Women don't have that ingredient. It's two steps somewhere, and one step somewhere else, and then it's time to eat, change one's mind, or vacate the mind. Sometimes I get no reading when I take a peek into their minds. I prefer action—cat simple and productive.

When we go places or meet John's friends, many are females. They coo over me, smell me, and often get their faces close to mine and try to kiss me, lick me, talk to me, or touch or feel me (no, not that way) in weird ways. For one thing, they have horrible smelling breath, and whatever they spray themselves with is worse than how people often describe cat's elimination. To make it worse, they touch my whiskers with theirs. (Yes, many have whiskers and lots of funky hair inside their noses as well.) I get an immediate mind-reading of stuff that I repeat to Al just to hear him laugh and do flips, and watch his newly inventive spin moves. (He stands on his hind feet, tippy toes to be exact, balancing on his tail, holds his paws high in the air, and twirls around like a whirling dervish, meowing constantly, while mixing in a growl, and once, he flatulated and then said he didn't mean it. But Al uses his "artistic license" upon occasion, like always.)

In retrospect and seeing what I have written, I must say, females might give me a glimmer of thought that such a vast expanse of zero nothingness is an actuality, and its size and whereabouts are completely unimaginable and undefinable, except, ahem, for which I have just described. I must say and give him praise that Uncle Al has a grasp of female mentality and his whirling dervish dance, farting, meowing, and hopping around with great speed on a roof high above and overlooking San Francisco one night was a start in the right direction. I watched intently as Al danced with great creativity, passion, and lust with reckless abandon! Al, alone, on that night would put the Bolshoi in a senior home. Warren Buffet declaring bankruptcy. Harlem on Malibu beach, feminists subscribing to *Hustler*. Dizzy Gillespie in a rowboat, Sinatra in Nebraska, the Pope in a synagogue, Picasso in an Andy Worhol exhibition, Hitler marrying Gloria Steinem, Genghis Khan at Big Sur, and the Moslems stocking up on Jimmy Dean hot dogs for a Christmas party, all cleanly shaved, in Brooks Brothers suits, telling jokes, putting bi-cycles together under the tree, and their wives in the kitchen making hot toddies, talking about Weight Watchers, and oh my, did Helen just get a divorce, and didn't I just see her heading to the Italian part of town?! Wink, wink, what a night!

Just then it started to rain, and we went our separate ways. Al jumped a seagull, and I only had a two-minute walk home. Hmmm, I better be careful. If John knew what I was up to, he would try to sell me to Hollywood for sure. As I often say, "Gotta keep a close eye on that guy."

Six-Toed Giant Cats

I may not have six toes, but I have absolutely everything else. (Don't be "catty" and say you don't have a driver's license as well. Okay, I will accept the gauntlet, and tell you neither did JFK, FDR, and for that matter, neither does the Pope.) Hemingway and Sinatra were crazy about cats with lots of digits. Then again, they were pretty much crazy about lots of anything. Ahem! I run into many of my cat friends from time to time, and most are totally unconcerned about anything.

One frightening exception is my giant relation in the zoos. One peek into their minds told me zoos should not be—not for big kitty cats, at least. The tiger and lions I "visited" wanted out, and they were ready to go in an instant. Very beautiful, but also very, very, very dangerous. Not a speck of that instinct in me. Of course, ahem, I have my mind, and if I wanted to be extremely dangerous, I well could be with that. Then again, someone with a book of matches could be also. Too much philosophy I see. Those big "kitty cats" sure gave me a wake-up call. My advice is to let them go and stay away, far, far away! Because I can read their minds, I know they want to eat you! Really!

Going to Paris!

*U*ncle Al came over to me in a big rush and announced his arrival by yelling out a large "MEOW!" I wanted to tell him to get a phone, but he is old-fashioned in some ways. Then again, he likes to scream as loud as he can at midnight. That's okay with me. He doesn't wake up John (who does), but then anyone else in the area would probably get up and go to the fridge for a quick one. He was more excited this time than usual, and that is quite a stretch, since he is usually full of something he got hold of out of one of his favorite restaurant "disposal units." Lately, he's been dining at Chez Paree, and I think they use lots of hormones in their fish to "soup up" their aging clientele and make them feel they have not "lost a step," ahem.

Chez Paree, I am sure, had Uncle Al fired up tonight. We met by our favorite chimney overlooking San Francisco "on a high and windy sea." Al said he flew over by pigeon express and complained about the size of the pigeon, saying it was hardly strong enough to make it to our favorite place. The poor pigeon was resting against the chimney and giving Al the "bird look." I always bring food, so I gave the pigeon some, and he cooed gratefully and muttered that in addition to Al wanting to ride all over the city at all hours, he also meows like crazy and never tips. I gave him five dollars and told him to wait around so that he could give me a ride home. We will call Seagull Express for Al. They are much bigger and faster, and they charge before they carry, just like American Airlines, tip included, and you get one stop along the way if you don't weigh over twenty pounds. Al will just make it, and he can yell all he wants because seagulls don't care about noise. They make a lot themselves, and may even chime in and do some dipsy diving to give Al more "spark."

Al and I got on top of the chimney, where it was nice and cozy, and Al even puffed on a small cigar. Al was so excited that great puffs of smoke came out of him as he meowed, pestered, and flicked his tail every which way, and batted the air constantly with his speedy paws. It all came down to this. Al was going to Paris! Would I check the shipping lanes for him so he would know when and where to fly? He said he preferred the warmer route, but he was in a big rush. What's new? He said he was ready right now, and that we should get a shipping route and get the show on the road, as he likes to say so well, and so often. I agreed, and I was very excited for him, and I asked why Paris? "It is the food," he said. "If it's this good here, just imagine what it will be like there!" His eyes were all aglow from the lights of the city and the warmth of the chimney and that cigar he was smoking. Or, the hormones he had recently ingested were making him all puffed up, and I wished for once in my life, I had a camera!

As an afterthought, he wanted to see "The Tower," as he called it, and take in some shows at the Moulin Rouge. Wealthy clientele go there and frequently drop things he needs, usually expensive jewelry, and he sells them for anybody's guess. (Probably Havana cigars and 24-hour Seagull Service—I mean he gets everything else free! Then again, what cat doesn't?) We went immediately to an all-night newspaper stand, and I got the shipping routes and times while Al was walking around on his hind feet and meowing out loudly "The Star-Spangled Banner" so as to keep the clerk distracted. It worked. (Then again, everything we do does.) But he more than distracted the man. He scared him, and the man was soon on the phone, trying to get Animal Control. (Good luck! I thought. If they show up, and he tells them what he saw, they will put him in the pound.) Just to give Al an extra edge, I supplied him with a cat car jacket with lots of pockets full of cigars and matches. I was going to take him to the 49er's locker room and "borrow" some "pain pills" and explain that these are just as good as goose liver and pig ribs loaded with hormones, butter, and salt. But why rain on a St. Paddy's Day parade of one happy cat? Uncle Al was joyous beyond belief! He loved the orange cat car jacket, cigars and matches, and what he was thinking and imagining all at once would triple fill the Harvard Law Library and the Library of Congress. Then again, you must remember, he is a cat, but it was still very terrific! We jumped up on our hind legs and meowed and cat-batted the air, and I even had a few puffs.

I read in the paper and heard on Coast to Coast the next day that UFOs had landed on the wharf. They had taken over the bodies of two huge cats and injected them with a fearsome drug until they turned orange and lost complete control of their bodies. In the middle of this frenzied activity, the story went on to say, a giant raptor emitting an ear-piercing cry, which was mixed in with the mournful wailing of the two UFO orange cat bodies, swooped down in the blink of an eye and took them out to sea. Some say the sound reminded them of Kate Smith's "God Bless America" juggernaut of a song. Those who said it were questioned and proved highly unreliable, drunk as well, while lying on their backs and telling of this UFO sound and laughing way too much. They were taken to the Buena Vista, best place in the city, supplied with much Irish coffee, and all there who heard the story and imbibed in the greatest coffee in San Francisco danced away, laughing uncontrollably, and concluded without a doubt that the Irish had returned as singing orange cats, and that now it was every man for himself. Watch out, Paris!

London

I love London. Perfect for cats and plenty of places to hide. Must be five million other cats here, and I know where all the good restaurants are. I met Seagull Joe right after we landed, and we began looking for mink coats. A huge shipment had been stolen, and our cigars along with them. We figured it was easier to find a fur coat and find out where it came from than to check on all the puffers in London. It seems like everything is smoking something. It didn't take long to find a mink coat, and all we had to do was take a close-up look to see if it was the brand we were looking for. It was. It was a man's mink coat, ankle length, top of the line, and must have been worth about $300k. The guy who wore it was smoking one of MY cigars. He was a very big man, around seven feet tall and weighing 340. (How humans get so big I will never know.) We decided to follow him, and hopefully he would lead us to what we wanted to know. It's easy for a cat to follow somebody, especially when you have eyes in the sky. If I lost the guy in the mink coat, Joe would always tell me where he went. The big man lumbered along at an easy pace, with great puffs of smoke seemingly coming out of the mink coat. He had an umbrella opened over his head which captured the smoke, making it all look like a giant mink coat moving down the sidewalk with a dark cloud on top. He was headed for the Savoy, and within five minutes, he had checked in his umbrella, mink coat, and palmed $20 to the checker, and then went over to the bar. It was easy for me to get in because the mink coat was the same color as mine. I walked right along with the coat and went in with The Giant.

While walking with the mink coat and The Giant, I used my mind-reading powers. He was a giant, and he had giant plans. He was the leading underworld figure in London and much of Europe. He had control of all of the shipping in and out of London, and could get or "bargain" for whatever he wanted. It just so happened that this week, he wanted mink coats and cigars. Upon offloading the cigars and mink coats, he stored them in one of his warehouses on the docks, and none was the wiser, that is, until Joe and I and about a thousand of my friends went to find where they were stored. The word went out to all the dock cats, and they told me shortly in lightning fast cat talk where everything was. There was way more than mink coats and cigars, they also reported. The warehouse was as long and wide as two football fields, and it was full of everything you could imagine, including tons of canned tuna fish. You can imagine how excited the dock cats were. Nuts to the cigars and coats and ivory and TVs; they wanted the canned tuna fish.

Since John was along busily doing nothing in London, except enjoying himself, I went back to our hotel room. When he arrived, I made it be known (letting him think it was his idea, ahem) where the cigars might be, and how to get them back. John smiled, what I sometimes think is almost a Chinese cat smile, petted me, put me in his backpack, and off we went. We booked an empty charter plane that would leave at a moment's notice, and went to London's best repertoire theatre. We signed up twenty-five actors dressed as Bobbies and explained *most* of what was happening. (If only my dear old Dad could see me now. Surely, Mom would not approve!) Seagull Joe and who knows how many of his friends decided to come along for the ride when they found about the canned "tuny" pronounced "toon-ee." They covered a good portion of the dock warehouse and quietly waited for the Bobbies to arrive.

One half hour later, the Bobbies showed up with a number of eighteen-wheelers, and the show began. The doors to the warehouse were opened, and the thugs took off like they were on fire. Joe Seagull and his buddies bombed them continually until they were clear of the docks, and by that time, all was loaded into the trucks. We got the cigars and a couple of mink coats. The actors were paid off handsomely, and the seagulls got the tuna they were craving. Not to be selfish, and besides, it was difficult for a seagull to use a can opener, so they bombed away with the tuna cans all over the dock area where my faithful furry friends were watching with great anticipation. Thousands of tuna cans banged, crunched, and slammed down onto the hard dock roads, and it was a wild "tuny" time cat and seagull jamboree.

On the front page news of the venerable *London Times*, it was reported that thousands of cats and birds for as long as the great paper had ever printed the news got along fabulously for about half a day, sharing tons of canned tuna fish that had been dropped from the sky. In the center of this tuna from heaven downpour was a mysterious warehouse that was stuffed with many shipments that had been stolen over the years. It was the work of The Giant, but could not be proven. Later the next day, The Giant was arrested for standing naked on top of Big Ben and yelling at the seagulls. Guess he must have had a cigar with too much catnip in it. You think? (British humor is so understated.)

The great helpers of mine were so happy. As we took off from Heathrow with our good-gotten gain, John and I looked at the airfield below. It was completely covered with cats and seagulls, and a few tuna cans here and there. All of them were smoking the Coco

Cabana Cha Cha Cigars. Meowing, cawing, waving their append-age of choice, and singing somewhat in unison "The White Cliffs of Dover." I could be wrong, but it brought a tear or two to my whiskers. John looked at me with a knowing smile, gave me a can of tuna, and said, "I love that song, ahhhh!"

Night of the Tunnels

$\mathcal{F}$ ire engines, sirens, honking, lights flashing—there was bedlam in the air. We were out for an evening stroll—well, John was—and I was in my backpack observing the beautiful San Francisco night in Little Italy. I had my paws on either side of John's head, and I was moving my head back and forth, trying not to miss a thing. A song went through my head about San Francisco, and I was ecstatic, "Sitting on the dock of the bay wasting time." It was written at the end of Columbus Street by Otis Redding, not far from where we were. We began following the lights and sounds. We wanted to observe things first paw, if you will. Although I can read minds and foresee the future, I don't always do it. After all, I am a cat, and genius cat or not, I still do a lot of what cats do. Nothing...

In fifteen minutes we were standing outside of the Fairmont Hotel, one of the greatest hotels in the world. It was surrounded by fire engines, police cars, and you name it. Something was going on, and we wanted to know what it was. Just so happened, a few of my furry brethren were close by, and as John sat down to watch, I asked what had happened. They told me a heavy shipment of some sort had been brought in, and shortly thereafter had fallen right through the cement floor into a tunnel directly beneath the Fairmont. Upon further investigation, the tunnel was found to go under the Fairmont and kept going all over Nob Hill. It didn't stop there. The tunnel kept going until it and other runoff tunnels had covered most of San Francisco. What a discovery! But there was something sinister about the tunnels as well. There were bodies strewn throughout the tunnels as they wound their way past and under many of the great businesses in the world, including the banks. Aha! The game was afoot! (I can't say apaw and plagiarize one of the most famous of Sherlock Holmes' statements, not yet at least.) Many "coincidences" were now being brought to light. Throughout the years, many unexplained robberies had happened, with the robbers seemingly disappearing into thin air. When apparently, they had actually gone into the tunnels.

I immediately got the word out to all the cats in the San Francisco area and told them what I wanted them to do, with free sardines and cigars, of course. If it was a big discovery, there would be more sardines and cigars. Cats are simple in some ways but we like lots. The mission of all the cats was to find every tunnel in the Great City, and then tell me where they were and what was in them. Pure cat's play, for in half a night, I had the entire schemata of all the tunnels in the city and their history.

About 160 years ago, when The Great City was being built and the cross-continental railroad was doing so as well, there were two significant gangs in the area, The Green Men and The Tong, Irish and Chinese. They built tunnels everywhere, so as not to bring attention to themselves. (Haven't the Irish changed since then, but the Chinese not so much?) After all was seemingly under control and the great constructions had been accomplished, the tunnels continued to flourish more than ever. They fit in perfectly with all the easy crime jobs that could be committed and apparently still do. I just had to find out what was going on! Curiosity and cats go paw in paw, don't you know? The gangs were different now. They were led by the Russians. They simply did whatever in the crime world they wanted to do. They had carte blanche to every major business in the city.

Now what? I decided, after a chimney talk with my friends and cohorts against crime, slime, and you name it. We met on a roof overlooking the city by a chimney that gave us a 360-degree view and was found to be one of the "power spots" on the planet. "We" being mainly my Uncle Al, Seagull Joe, and about thirty of my furry brethren, all of whom were glad to run errands and help shore up our plans and schemes. (I must add, my furry brethren, although enthusiastic and eager, were not fully developed and at times got carried away when sent on an errand, like the time we were looking into a container ship caper. They mistook a high-profile passenger ship for what we wanted, ate all the caviar, returned completely bloated, and said everything was purrrr-fect! We now used them as an example of what not to do.)

The Russians were planning on one of the biggest crimes the world has ever known. (Discounting wars.) They were going to steal the entire gold shipment of the West Coast, about a trillion dollars is all. I had a hunch most of it would end up in Putin's hands or paws or banks or maybe under his bed. No doubt, however, in my humble cat's opinion, he may be another creep, and no matter how much money he will ever have, he will never be welcomed outside of the stone-cold walls where he and his lackeys scrounge about. (Thank you for listening to my completely objective judgment about a creep and his keepers. Harrumph!)

I immediately told John all that was "going down". (I try to be current with all these supposed slang terms that eventually end up in the dictionary. Doesn't mean I like 'em much. More harrumphs.) Stalwart authorities, by that, I mean people who were not politically affiliated, were told, and the Russians, these Russians, were squashed like the bugs they were and imprisoned forever. Most were also found to be murderers and thieves. The stolen loot was restored. Some we will never know where it went. Ahem!

Whenever John and I go for a stroll on San Francisco Bay, I will always remember the night of the tunnels. A cat's dream all messed up by lawless, lazy men. We now use the tunnels for whatever we want. Mostly wagging our tails and giving us shortcuts to the various sardine shipments down on the docks. I must admit I do not share their love of sardines. What's a cat to do? There is simply no accounting for taste.

It's Just Another Day

*A*liens are a big subject wherever you go. I have never seen one, nor had anybody tell me they had seen one. But so much had been talked about them that I thought it was time to look into the matter. What better friends to ask and get info from than my good friends, Uncle Al and Seagull Joe. As usual we met by the warm chimney on a bright and sunny San Francisco day, sparkling throughout. So apparently were Uncle Al and Seagull Joe. I told them about the aliens and asked if they could give me any help regarding such a thing, if there was even a thing at all. Joe said he would ask around, and since around to him meant about five million birds, I thought that was a good start. Al said, "I will contact all the brethren in the city, and all around it, and if we don't come up with any aliens, that means there are none. Some of my buddies are from the East Coast, and they are into everything."

Joe said, "While you are asking them about aliens, you might want to mention paying their taxi fares. Some young cat thought he was going to stiff me for the fare, and I dropped him off at about one hundred feet over the bay. He was only fifty yards from shore." Everyone understood. Cigars were lit and Seagull Joe took off, leaving a beautiful trail of blue-gray smoke with a hint of some exotic scent. Al said he would do his usual, and if there were any aliens, he and his would know about it. Al said to me, "What are these aliens doing, and what do they look like?"

I said, "Most people say they are about four feet tall with gray coloring, and look like Barney Fife naked. Some say they are kidnapped and taken into a kind of a hideout, and later find themselves lying almost anywhere. Reports from the military say they never have heard of such a thing and Area 51 doesn't exist."

We went our separate ways, and later the next day Seagull Joe had a cat fare almost next door, so he stopped by and gave his five million bird report. Joe said, "The damn things are all over! The trouble is that the split second you see them, they change into whatever else they want or they disappear altogether. One tried to get a fare with me yesterday, but when he reminded me so much of Barney Fife, I was laughing so hard I had to land. By that time, he had turned into a fire hydrant. I knew because a dog was about to pay a visit, then yelped and ran away."

Uncle Al and his legions said they were all over San Francisco, looking this way or that way, and moving so fast that it was hard to keep up with them. One crazy younger kitten thought it was some kind of a joke and jumped on one alien by the ball park. It immediately turned into a bulldog, and now the kitten will never go near a dog again.

Aliens were about. Now we knew. What to do? The plan was simple and direct as all good plans are. There are many big cats around The City who were contacted and showed up by evening at the chimney meeting place at the stroke of midnight. Cigars were passed all around. (We had quite a few since the two-billion-dollar deal with Castro, so we dispensed them freely, knowing it would take about a hundred years before we even put a dent in all the cigars we had lying around.) Soon puffs of smoke enveloped not only the chimney, and us cats, but also the entire top of the house. (I could see we might have to rethink the complimentary cigar, or keep it under fifty anyhow.) I told Al and the other cats the plan, and much meowing, purring, tail wagging, air cat-batting, whisker wiping, and such went on. Of course, a few fell asleep and then, I knew the plan was afoot.

When the big cats stretched out and stood on their hind legs, they were at least four feet tall. By now they knew what the plan was going to be, and a few started yelling out, "Andy, where are you?" It was too funny, 'nuff to make a cat laugh. The plan went into effect immediately. The big cats went about the city looking like four-foot Barney Fifes trying to meet a lookalike. In two hours we had met ten and brought them all to the meeting house, which was the chimney. A couple of cats brought in another cat, which just goes to prove how slick those aliens are. Or, maybe those cats were one cigar over the limit. (They smell so great, and cats love 'em.) The aliens were hard to handle as they kept transforming themselves into all kinds of things, and it was tough to keep them pinned down, but not for Uncle Al. He just fogged them, and they returned to their four-foot Barney Fife selves, and we began to talk. Every now and then I would hear someone cry out, "Andy, where are you?" and we had a fantastic time! The aliens told us the entire story. They were just traveling, actually "exploring," around the planet Earth and decided to visit some of the living things on the ground. Reactions were varied, but no one was hurt, and would someone please tell them what "Andy, where are you?" means?

One thing led to another, and Al, being the consummate sales cat that he is, told them he had "such a deal" for them. They listened, they smoked, and they were entranced. Al showed them a little of the Cuban rumba, air cat-batting, and a few choice meows. The aliens caught on quickly, and by the time they left had concocted a Cuban rumba song that went, "Andy, where are you, cha cha cha!" One of the younger cats was laughing so hard, he fell off the roof, but Seagull Joe picked him right out of the air, took him home, and got his fare. (I think I have to keep a closer eye on Seagull Joe.) Of course, as in any sale, there must be a payment for goods. We asked what they could trade back to us, and they asked, "What do you want?" We told them. They gave us what we wanted and each parted their happy ways, looking forward to seeing each other here and there. As they slowly left, I could still hear the "cha cha cha" song in the background being blown about by the San Francisco windy sea. All of a sudden we heard a swooshing sound. We could not see a thing, except for a huge blue-gray cloud disappearing into nowhere. It was reported in all the media that a strange blue-gray cloud had passed over The City in the blink of an eye. A small article on page 19 of *The Chronicle* reported that all high-rise window washers had to take the day off immediately after the cloud passed over. They complained of being "too high" all of a sudden, and someone was thought to have heard them singing "cha cha cha"! So much for page 19 articles, it was said, and so foolish when there are so many more important things to report about.

Kiss Me

asey, my cat, keeps doing crazy things. The song on the radio went like this, "Kiss me once, and kiss me twice, and kiss me once again…" When Casey heard that song, he looked at me and gave me a huge cat smile. At least, I think it was. He knew I liked that song because he would hear me singing it around the house, and he must have liked it too. (Casey considers himself a man, er, cat about town.) I laughed and sang along as I always did, and he did a few pirouettes and then had to get a drink of water…typical. Me, I was ready for a Samuel Adams beer after all that singing.

Now it was time to pack and get on the ship to Honolulu. I had lived there before and knew something about it, and I had heard there was trouble in dreamland. It wasn't the usual drug or some other phooey problem. It was some type of a plan to get a foothold on the planet Earth. Strategically, Honolulu is at the center of the planet, so in theory, whoever has Honolulu has the world as we know it.

I must tell you again that Casey is not an ordinary cat. For openers, he is telepathic and can read minds. How do I know? He tells me. He has decided that I am the one he will communicate with. I am his conduit to humans. He tells me what is really going on, and I must act upon the information. I guess he chose me because he likes me, simple as that. It is why we have pets, friends, and lovers, because we like them. He knew that I was the purrfect person to help him. Casey is a heavy hitter.

The Hawaiian Islands have many mountainous areas that no one has ever seen. It was in that area that the evil turmoil began to take place. The evildoers were going to turn the world upside down by flipping the night sky topsy-turvy so that they could complete their evil mission. They were going to enslave the planet Earth. If one can rearrange the sky and take away our base of zero bearing, we are put in a hopeless situation. They know we will give anything to get it back. What else? Crude, but true, if we don't have our night sky as we know it, we won't know our boo-boo from a hole in the ground.

* * *

Honolulu was great! I was with John in my usual spot, his back-pack. We went walking up and down the beach, and had a great time at the beach hangouts, with John telling his "fantastic" comedic stories, as always, kidding around. Some remembered him being in Honolulu before, and being very funny. I helped things out by inter-preting in their minds what John was really saying, and that saved John's reputation, so they didn't take things with the wrong inten-tions. We certainly didn't need to get involved in a beach sand flying brawl without our reinforcement backup crew along. We went to an open beach bar right on the water. The sound of the waves sometimes smacked against the seawall ten feet from where we were sitting. As usual, some folks at the bar asked what John was doing with that cat in the backpack. John showed them my orange care cat jacket and the pockets that held his prescriptions, and then they all laughed and understood. They wanted to get closer to see me better, which was fine with John, but he told them, "Casey is shy, so you must under-stand." (Me, shy? Oh boy, the blarney was starting to fly already!) John put me on the giant round bar counter, which must have been one hundred feet around, and said, "Here he is!" I sat shyly on the bar and then slowly walked back and forth with a meow or two. Of course, everyone in the bar had their eyes on me, and I waved my tail and sniffed the air as they expected a cat to do. Unbeknownst to them, I was also, since I can read minds, listening to what they were thinking. Jackpot! John was right, there was trouble in dreamland! But I couldn't stop now. I had to keep acting like some kind of a show cat, so I did what a show cat does. (How I learned to be a show cat, you can find out later, pretty silly). I proceeded to walk around the one hundred foot bar with my tail high in the air, smiling, meowing, winking, and giving it the old kitty hind kick now and then, with a good cat-bat or two mixed in. A little Uncle Al boxing tactic kept their eyes fascinated with me. Every now and then, I would stop and kiss a pretty lady's cheek or hand. They absolutely adored me. While doing this terrific cat walk caper, dodging glasses of wine, drinks, and bottles of beer, I was also secretly seeing into everyone's minds. Very interesting, this technique! The most interesting part being that some of the people there were able to read minds as well. Uh oh! Gave me quite a fright, and I jumped quickly in the backpack so John would know it was time to make a move out of there, pronto! I advised John who the suspicious people were, and what their thoughts and plans were all about, which sounded extremely dangerous. They were hours away from changing the sky into so many positions that we would all be lost. There would be no more North Star or any kind of star constellation we were familiar with. The world would all become one total chaotic mess, and we would all crash without our stars to navigate and give us direction.

Okay, I knew I had to do something fast. I decided to use my beauty to captivate them. I jumped out of the backpack and stood on my hind feet and began to do a cat dance around the hundred-foot bar. All the cheering, clapping, whining, yelling, and "Oh boy, what a cat!" were music to my ears. Actually, I was doing a cat dance that would enslave and hypnotize their minds, making them do my absolute bidding with gusto! Can't believe how beautiful I was. On my two back feet, I whirled and twirled, jumped and pirouetted, waved my sexy tail, and cat-batted the air in rhythm with the music of the band playing. I was cookin'! (Making an ass out of myself really, but I had a job to be done lightning fast.) The night became a dream of dreams come true, as so many couples looked at me and were in a world of loving awe. They were so entranced with my dancing and cat-batting that they knew this was truly a time of all times. (Ah, tourists—we love them in Honolulu.)

After two, yes, two times around the bar, with my delicate cat dancing, meowing, and throwing in a loud purr here and there (once I gave it a tiger growl, but I had to be careful since there were lots of real tigers down there, and they were all jealous), I had the crowd hypnotized as cats have been doing to people for eons. They loved me completely, wanted me, but knew I was unobtainable because I was much too beautiful with too much talent. (Their subconscious, what there was of it after being hypnotized, said only a yin yang could be that beautiful and talented. They didn't exactly say yin yang either…ahem.) The crowd around the large bar was deliriously happy with joy, knowing they were witnessing a great show. (Sure made some of the guys horny.) Three people looked at me like poison, and they were not entertained. They were only there researching how to kill and confuse all of us. My hypnosis hadn't worked on them apparently, which was extremely odd. They must've been immune, which had never happened in my experiences before.

"No problem," I told John. (John has "big connections" in Honolulu, as he likes to say). He made a few phone calls to his *big connections*. I kept dancing to work the hypnosis effect on all the others until some Hawaii Five O and Magnum types came in

and picked those creeps up without anyone noticing. Suddenly, their plans were finished for good, and the world and the constellations were saved. I was almost tired, and it was only midnight. I had just danced more than two times around a hundred-foot bar, and saved the world, too. John was laughing while I was falling asleep. I just hoped he wouldn't tell me any more jokes that would keep me awake. I let him know to go easy on what is 'nuff to make a cat laugh. Sure...I needed one long catnap. To think it all started with that song, 'Kiss me once, and kiss me twice..."
ZZZZZZZZzzzzzzzzzzzzzzzzzzzzzzzz

I Love Paris in the Springtime!

*J*ohn and I went to Paris. It was springtime, and John felt that he had to go, and imagine what he thought the song "I Love Paris in the Springtime" really meant. Okay, so off we went, first class, of course, compliments of my cat care jacket stuffed with pills to help the old boy keep whatever he has health-wise. As for me, with my all-encompassing abilities of mind-reading and the most gifted mind in the universe, all that was required of me was to go along for the ride, in a cat's meow. We had the best seats and the most attention. I, being the most beautiful cat anyone had ever seen, and John, speaking blarney at a comfortable rate, made us great travelers. We were, of course, in first class, with all we could eat, and that's about it. John eats like a bird. I know, birds eat a lot, and I eat whatever I want. I also do whatever I want. I have lots of backup. If I need to tell you, I will. My backup is everywhere, in the sky and on the ground. And, of course, John doing and telling me things that are 'nuff to make a cat laugh. Remember the movie *The Saint* with Roger Moore, and the song they played throughout? Well, play it now. It will fit in perfectly. Come on now, play it in your mind. After all, your mind is what this is all about anyhow. What? (Always loved that British expression, "What?" especially when Watson or Sherlock Holmes would say it. 'Nuff to make a cat sigh.)

As usual I had to "clear the area," that is, make sure we were safe. Simple for me to do. All I had to do was to take a look into the various minds, and I use the term loosely in many cases, and "see" what was going on. Not much and "What?" as good old Wattie would say, "What have we here?" I must answer the "What?" that Watson would ask by saying as Sherlock would answer, "Evil, old boy, evil." The game was definitely afoot. It would not happen on the plane but in Paris. If the evil plan succeeded, Paris would never be the same, and I don't mean like a smashing play that would grab the hearts of all everywhere. (Even a cat must take literary license at times. I must admit, I took it. Now, back to the "Evil.") There were four people in various seats of first class. (Their first mistake! Crooks can never hobnob with the commoners, don't cha know?) They were the detonators of the pile of dynamite that was in Paris that they would ignite and bring down, you guessed it, The Eiffel Tower.) How common, all the scum of the world had tried to do it, but these criminals had a significantly more sophisticated plan. They were going to shapeshift themselves as parts of the Tower, and voila, blow it all to smithereens! (Love the word "smithereens" and every cat wants to say it. Now, I have done it. Cats all over the world will smile when they find out it has been written down, and that it is their favorite word. Heaven help us if they all meow at once. Purring would be more heavenly! Both combined would put the world in ecstasy forever. Humph, can't have that! What? Good ole Watson and all. So much joy! Not to worry. Several cats will be staring at a falling star and that will be that, plenty of time for cat ecstasy. Cats have ecstasy all the time, so... It would take too much to help you understand, and besides, we must get on with the Eiffel Tower shape shifters.)

I looked into their evil minds and found out what they were going to do. It was a good plan and a dangerous plan. They would shapeshift into a part of the tower, and upon synchronization, would all at once go...kaboom! Eiffel Tower coming down. Seemingly easy enough to stop, but even if one slightly suspected, the jig was up, as it were. (Isn't it great to hear those descriptive expressions once more?) One of the shape shifters would trip the switch, and all would be blown from wherever they were. They had to be snuffed out. Lots of snuff for these stinkers and I had just the plan. I would stuff the snuffers. Meow! Throw in a purr or two as well, make it lots of purrs, because I like the Tower. As it is with most evil people, they were going to celebrate before they completed their dastardly mission. (Couldn't hardly celebrate afterward, now, could they? 'Nuff to make a cat laugh! Meow!) They were going to celebrate a night of frivolity on the great river of Paris, the Seine. They were going to party all night and at midnight, so fitting for these ne'er-do-wells, get off on their specially charted boat and go to the Eiffel tower, and then kaboom! They would shapeshift into one of the feet of the Tower, detonate simultaneously, and the Eiffel Tower would be coming down. (Using a cat's literary license once more, and, yes, I am aware we only have only nine licenses. Maybe I used up two on this one. Okay, give me three. Harrumph!)

The plan began. The boat was rented and directions were given. Party, party, party, and then at ten minutes until midnight, they would disembark and taxi to the Eiffel Tower. (So beautiful and so evil.) John was "told" of the plan, and that he would be the pilot. I would be one of the Paris cats that were usually on many boats of this nature. At exactly fifteen minutes before midnight while we were in the deepest part of the Seine river, the "rent a boat" took a sudden deep dive. Sixty feet down and all were submerged, except for me and John. The evil people were so confused, since this was their first mission and all, they tripped the detonator switch. Boom! Biggaboom! Only a slight smuff and wuffle on top of the water;

underneath, who knows? The death of another devil as we all know. (Sometimes it is necessary to answer rhetorical questions. Don't want to be too mysterious. Even cats can overdo it.)

John and I were on the fashionable Left Bank by the great church of Notre Dame, being celebrated by our survival by all around, still soaking wet. I was giving John thoughts of the time he tried to play football in college for Notre Dame, which actually never happened. We just saved the Eiffel Tower, and what was John doing? He was making his football moves in mime. Making a cat do what they rarely do. 'Nuff to make a cat laugh!

Playing Cards

X Playing Cards

X Getting money—Al got it

X Went to San Francisco

X Stopped and picked up cousins Sophia & Bridgett

X Met Murph the tiger

X Put all people on telepathic communication

    ... $\mathcal{S}$o we knew what each one was thinking and saying, exactly like a conversation and more, because we could convey our thoughts and emotions between all of us at once. I heard their thoughts telepathically, and meanwhile not a sound was made, but I could tell Murph wanted to growl out big time once in a while. Of course, Al was getting itchy to hitch a ride on a seagull. Bridgett and Sophia's thoughts were universally impossible to describe. I will leave it to you what they thought, almost overwhelming even for me, definitely for Al, positively delirious, and the girls loved it. Al and I will have to get more money for John to have plastic surgery to get the smile off his face, and dare I meow, that ain't all! Ahem! 'Nuff to make a cat laugh!

www.ingramcontent.com/pod-product-compliance
Lightning Source LLC
Chambersburg PA
CBHW031309280626
47169CB00017B/1088